ESCALATION

ESCALATION

RICK BARBA

INSIGHT
EDITIONS

San Rafael, California

INSIGHT EDITIONS

PO Box 3088
San Rafael, CA 94912
www.insighteditions.com

 Find us on Facebook: www.facebook.com/InsightEditions
Follow us on Twitter: @insighteditions

Library of Congress Cataloging-in-Publication Data available.

ISBN: 978-1-60887-992-2

PUBLISHER: RAOUL GOFF
ASSOCIATE PUBLISHER: VANESSA LOPEZ
ART DIRECTOR: CHRISSY KWASNIK
DESIGNER: YOUSEF GHORBANI
SENIOR EDITOR: MARK IRWIN
MANAGING EDITOR: ALAN KAPLAN
EDITORIAL ASSISTANT: MAYA ALPERT
PRODUCTION EDITOR: RACHEL ANDERSON
PRODUCTION MANAGERS: ALIX NICHOLAEF | GREG STEFFEN

COVER ART BY ALEX GARNER

ROOTS of PEACE   REPLANTED PAPER

Insight Editions, in association with Roots of Peace, will plant two trees for each tree used in the manufacturing of this book. Roots of Peace is an internationally renowned humanitarian organization dedicated to eradicating land mines worldwide and converting war-torn lands into productive farms and wildlife habitats. Roots of Peace will plant two million fruit and nut trees in Afghanistan and provide farmers there with the skills and support necessary for sustainable land use.

Manufactured in the United States by Insight Editions

10 9 8 7 6 5 4 3 2 1

After all, if you do not resist the apparently inevitable, you will never know how inevitable the inevitable was.

—*Terry Eagleton*

CONTENTS

ESCALATION

1

REAPER

LIGHTLY, ALMOST LOVINGLY, Alexis Petrov slid her index finger across the Vektor's trigger. Its carbonitride coating provided the perfect lubricity for moments like this. With a pull weight adjusted down to just six-and-a-half ounces, the slightest tap would send a copper-jacketed round burrowing straight through a target at one thousand meters per second.

"Step into the light, you slimy little bastards," she whispered.

Eye to scope, Petrov waited hungrily on targets six hundred meters below. Her mouth, dry for so long, moistened. A thin Pavlovian film of saliva thickened her tongue. Her stomach gnawed with both hunger and hatred. *The enemy is food.*

A deep voice off to her right mumbled something incoherent.

"What's that, CK?" she called.

"I don't like it," growled a big man, straddling a boulder on the rock ledge. He was sighting through his rifle's optics too.

"They been in there, what, an hour? Place is deserted ten years now." He spat. "The hell they looking for?"

CK Munger was a large mound of a man. In his meaty hands, even a bulky laser rifle looked like an elaborate toy. Few Reapers had such girth. Size like his typically didn't work well in the highlands where they operated. But CK could traverse a rockslide like a puma. It was an amazing thing to see.

Petrov turned to her left. "What you got, Natter?"

"Nothing, chief." Jean Natter was a petite woman with the voice of a little girl. But you didn't want her tracking you. Not if she was hungry.

Suddenly, CK whispered, "Yo, here we go!"

Below, three Sectoids emerged one by one from a half-collapsed A-frame chalet. Two were old-time Xrays, just a meter high. The other was new-breed more than twice their height. Petrov's scope view put her right in their midst. The bastards could sense something, she could tell. They crouched and moved warily. But their psionic reach did not extend six hundred meters.

"Three tangos, marked," she said quietly.

"Yeah, mark three," called CK.

"One, two, three," whispered Natter.

Petrov's rifle team was well-trained. Even basic field intel got multiple confirms.

CK spat again and looked over at her. "What do you think, chief?" he asked.

"We go hot," said Petrov.

"Roger that." CK sounded happy.

"I got left," said Natter. "Head shot, fool."

CK cackled. "Yoda is all head, pardner," he said. "You can't miss." He rotated his eye socket tighter into his scope. "Okay, so I go right," he said.

Petrov nodded grimly.

"I'm on the gollum, dead center," she called.

She put her crosshairs on the new-breed's nasty, grinning head. She rubbed the slick Elite trigger gently.

"On my call," said Petrov.

"Ready."

"Ready."

Petrov exhaled slowly. "Now."

* * *

Aliens did not look appetizing at first glance. Not by classic human standards anyway.

Petrov remembered the first time she field-dressed a Muton. The smell almost knocked her unconscious. Properly seasoned and prepared, however, Muton meat was remarkably tender and tasty. Some Reapers of American descent called it "roast beast," flashing back to their prewar Dr. Seuss childhoods.

But Sectoids presented entirely different culinary problems.

For one, the skin was tough as duck canvas, which made sense, considering the buggers ran around essentially naked, regardless of weather. But equally off-putting was Sectoid bodily fluid. Once you finally cracked open the skin, the steamy yellow slime that poured out looked like something leaking from a head gasket.

Amazingly, it made an excellent gravy.

"Natter, get those giblets bagged," said Petrov.

"Hurrying, chief," replied Natter. She was shoveling dirt over the dressing stains on the ground with her entrenching spade.

"Skip that," said Petrov. "We need to scoot before these guys are missed." She glanced up the ridgeline. "I don't like this."

"Why?"

"Not sure yet."

CK emerged from the chalet. "Nothing," he said. "Not a goddamned thing."

Petrov wiped her gutting knife, folded it shut, and slid it into a utility pocket. She said, "They were in there forever, CK."

"I know, man."

"What were they doing?"

CK gave her a look. "Resting," he said.

"Sectoids don't rest."

"I know." He shrugged.

Petrov slung a game bag over her shoulder. "Okay, whatever," she said. "Let's get this meat back to camp."

As CK scooped up the other game bag, Natter sealed a plastic pouch full of Sectoid organs and slipped it into her field pack. Reapers took a lot of pride in their economies—of motion, scale, action, resourcing, and consumption. Nothing wasted, not even the viscera. And they usually covered up their kill sites.

But Petrov felt edgy.

"Move out," she said.

Fifteen years in the Wild Lands had taught her to respect edgy feelings.

* * *

They hauled their kill down the old Shadow Canyon Trail right under Devil's Thumb.

It was a cool, cloudless mid-autumn day. Gaps in the tree line gave glimpses of New Denver's luminescent towers rising forty miles to the east. The new city had been erected adjacent to the old one, now a toxic pit and mass grave. Some estimates put one hundred thousand bodies sealed under the resin dome that covered fifty square miles of old Denver's downtown and residential districts.

"So many sheep," said CK, gazing east at the skyline.

"But I bet they sleep well," said Petrov.

CK hefted his game bag. "Hey, I sleep like a baby," he said.

Natter stared at the new city with dark eyes. "I want to slaughter them all and eat their children," she said in her little girl's voice.

This cracked up Petrov. "Jesus, Natter," she said.

Natter looked at her. "I hate them so much," she said.

"Why?"

"They're cowards."

Petrov turned to continue down the trail. "Not sure that's fair."

"They gave up," said Natter, falling in behind. "Just like XCOM did."

This was the general outlook among Reaper regulars: XCOM had been weak, a dismal failure. Under pressure, the vaunted agency had folded like a cheap dome tent.

"You're what, twenty-one?" asked Petrov.

Natter shrugged. "Don't really know."

"What?!"

Natter tromped along a few steps, then said, "Somebody found me somewhere."

"So . . . you don't remember what it was like before the invasion."

"Nope."

"I do," said Petrov. "I'm thirty. My dad grew up in Chicago, but his people came from Bulgaria. He once told me his own father, my grandpa, did bad things in Sofia during the Soviet era." Her smile was crooked. "And said he'd do them all again no hesitation. Because it gave his family food and comfort."

"That sucks," said Natter.

Now CK chimed in. "Look, I get it, man," he said. "Most people can't do this, what we do." He gestured around them with his huge hands. "If I had starving little kids, yeah, I'd probably drag them into the New Cities too."

Petrov gave him a look. "But Natter would eat them."

CK frowned. "All of them?" he asked.

Natter nodded. "Yep," she said.

"But you'd kill me first, right?"

"Only if you're home."

* * *

It had been a busy summer for Resistance cells all along the Front Range.

Hostile patrols were pushing from New Denver way up into the higher passes, a troubling development. This uptick of activity followed a pattern. First, a few old-school alien shock troops—Sectoid, Muton, Chryssalid, maybe a few Floaters in support—would deploy into a settlement area and terrorize the locals.

Then a day or two later, a transport of ADVENT Troopers would drop into town.

They'd administer medical aid to any wounded settlers, distribute food and fresh water, act semihuman (which is of course what they were), then start recruiting in the New Cities. High country survivors were skeptical folk, leaning toward tinfoil-hat paranoia, so the recruitment effort rarely went well.

Boulder got the worst of it. Once an upscale university town, it had become a rundown cluster of fire-camps, hardscrabble havens for survivalists and other flinty Neanderthal types. ADVENT paid frequent visits and never left without conducting a few rigorous interrogations as well.

Word afterwards was always the same: They were digging for intel on XCOM.

Petrov found it insulting. She hadn't seen any sign of XCOM in years. The locals all knew that Reapers ran the show along the Front Range.

* * *

Petrov's team was part of a twenty-one-man hunting detachment sent out from New Samara, the governing encampment of the Reaper clan. All of the Reaper enclaves east of the Divide were stocking up for winter. The foray had been good so far: Elk, deer, and small game were back, just twenty years after large swaths of the Front Range had been blasted black and polluted by the war. Forests on the eastern slopes were no longer ashen or deathly silent.

Of course, venison was fine. But the Reaper taste for alien flesh—once the product of desperation—had undergone years of refinement. CK and Natter had been arguing over recipes for months.

As they humped around the ridge, the grand debate continued.

"You're insane," grunted CK. "How can you not like the stroganoff?"

"Because it's disgusting," said Natter.

"What's disgusting about it?"

Natter just looked at him.

"Come on!" howled CK. "You got something against Sectoid loin?"

"I love Sectoid loin," said Natter.

"So?"

"So why would you ruin it by adding sour cream?" said Natter. She shook her head. "That just nauseates me."

Petrov was gazing up at Devil's Thumb, a curved granite spire jutting 150 feet up from the shoulder of Bear Peak. It was as familiar a landmark as anything in Petrov's life. Raised in a Reaper camp in the moraines below the Indian Peaks, she'd passed the rock thumb dozens of times on supply runs down the Shadow Canyon North Trail to the Boulder settlements.

CK followed Petrov's gaze upward.

"Ever been up on that thing?" he asked. "I mean, like, up top?"

"Couple times," replied Petrov.

CK nodded. They stopped for a few seconds, looking at the Thumb.

"Tough climb?" he asked.

"Nah," said Petrov. "The approach up the talus there is harder than the climb itself." She squinted. Something looked different. "What's that?"

CK squinted too. "How would I know?" he said. "It's your thumb."

Petrov's eyes widened. "The hell?"

She slipped the game bag strap off her shoulder, then slid her Vektor rifle from its sling. Bringing the stock to her shoulder and the scope to her eye, Petrov focused the optics on the top of the Thumb.

"It's gone," she said.

"What is?" asked CK.

"Something big up there," she said. She lowered the rifle.

"A hawk maybe."

Petrov frowned. "I've never seen a ten-foot hawk," she said.

"Ten foot?"

"It was big," said Petrov.

She looked at Natter, then at CK. They clearly didn't know what to make of it. But then something seemed to strike Natter. She cocked her head.

Petrov noticed and asked, "What, Jeannie?"

Natter said, "You can probably sight the camp from up there."

They looked at each other for a second. Then Petrov started sprinting down the trail.

"Son of a bitch," she hissed.

They left the game bags behind.

2

HUNTER

GUNFIRE BEGAN CRACKLING in the distance before Petrov was even halfway around the ridge.

Their detachment's base camp was tucked a half mile up Shadow Canyon next to a creek on the back side of the ridgeline that included Devil's Thumb. The trail took a wide swing around the ridge before snaking up the canyon along the creek. As Natter pointed out, the top of the Thumb would likely provide a clean view of the camp.

It took ten long minutes to reach the creek. By that time, Petrov could hear screams up ahead too.

Terrible screams. Agonized.

Good god! she thought, the back of her neck crawling in alarm.

Using hand signals, Petrov directed CK and Natter to split and move up either side of the canyon. Pistols drawn, they dashed into the low scrub trees along opposite walls. Off to her left, Petrov spotted a rock shelf jutting upward from the side of the canyon. Scrambling up, she slid into a cleft behind a long-dead tree trunk stripped of bark.

Above, Devil's Thumb leaned over the canyon. Petrov slid her Vektor from its sling again and flipped it up to her shoulder. Using the Nightforce scope, she quickly aimed upward to scan the top of the spire and saw nothing. Then she tried sighting high ledges on either side of the canyon. But again, nothing.

Up the canyon, two quick rifle shots seemed to add final punctuation to the terrible howling, which suddenly stopped.

Now there was nothing but silence.

Petrov hoped that was a good sign. Other than two or three sentries posted up the canyon, her full detachment should have been manning the camp. Fifteen Reapers could punch evenly with an entire battalion of aliens or ADVENT Troopers. And any enemy force that size moving on the ground would've been marked by spotters long ago.

But the screaming unsettled her. It had been tortured, like a gut-shot animal.

Petrov could see Natter up ahead, still hugging the left wall of the canyon. The small woman dashed like a sparrow hawk from tree to boulder. It didn't appear that she'd spotted anything yet; she was glancing around, checking all directions. After a second, Natter darted out of visual contact. Trees in the steep canyon were stunted by shadow and the shallow bedrock, but they still cut off sight lines. So Petrov slipped her rifle back into the sling and drew her pistol too. Rolling off the shelf, she landed lightly on the ground and scuttled upstream along the creek.

Now the silence was disturbing. Petrov ducked behind an outcropping right on the creek bed. The campsite was still out of view, but she knew it was just around the bend about fifty meters ahead. She listened tensely for a few seconds. There was no sound at all.

Then a flash of movement across the creek caught her attention.

It was CK. Despite his bearish bulk, he slipped lightly around a boulder and whistled the Reaper tactical warning call, the two-note song of the mountain chickadee. Then he started flashing hand signals at someone across the canyon: *Flanked to your left.* Alarmed, Petrov leapt up and sprinted lightly up the creek, glancing at CK. When he spotted her advance, his eyes grew big.

He spun toward her and raised his hands in two quick signals: *Stop. Cover.*

Then the back of his head exploded in a red spray.

His body fell hard and heavy.

In the seven years that she'd known CK Munger, from the first day he wandered into camp looking for food and a chance to fight ADVENT, Petrov had never seen the big man fall hard or heavy. He moved with impossible grace, always.

As her eyes clouded red with rage, Petrov heard another scream.

It could only be Natter, that voice.

But like the previous screams, it had a guttural, inhuman resonance.

"No," murmured Petrov.

She holstered her pistol and crept to a thick cottonwood half submerged at the bend. Wielding her Vektor again eye to scope, she sighted upstream. In glacial increments, she leaned out from the trunk. Every inch she leaned out, the scope revealed more horror.

Reaper bodies were strewn across the camp. Some had been hit unawares—carrying a stew pot, stoking the fire, stepping out of a tent. Most were clearly fighting back or trying to. Gunned down behind rocks, trees, weapons in hand. Apparently, no location had provided sufficient cover. Nowhere was safe.

But an unlucky few suffered a different fate.

Three Reaper soldiers—Petrov's old friends, comrades in arms, family—had been incapacitated somehow. Then strung up—alive and conscious, from the looks frozen on their faces— and torn open.

Sickness and hatred gurgled in Petrov's throat.

As she swung the Vektor back and forth, seeking the target and vengeance, she heard a metallic *zing* directly above her head.

* * *

When Petrov woke, it was to oily darkness and a searing pain in her shoulders.

Chamois cloth wrapped her eyes and mouth. Her arms and legs were trussed above her to a horizontal game-pole propped by two boulders. She hung, belly down. Her body weight stretched her sockets to near dislocation. She tried to cry out, but her mouth was packed tight.

Most unsettling of all, she felt her midsection exposed. Her cloak, shirt, and leggings had been torn just enough to expose her abdomen from navel to sternum. She felt a chinook breeze on her skin there.

A voice above her spoke, so impossibly deep it sounded synthesized.

"I'd planned to gut you alive, like I did some of your brethren," it said casually. "But now, I think not."

Petrov felt herself rising as the pole was lifted. Her body was set on the ground, gently, belly down, relieving the burning in her shoulders. Then she felt the game-pole slide down her back as it was pulled free.

"I don't begrudge your kills," said the voice calmly. She felt its deep vibrato in her stomach. "My troops are little more than failed experiments."

Something massive clamped onto her forearm, and she felt her wrist bonds cut free. The vice grip yanked her to a sitting position as if she were a rag doll. Then her ankle bonds were sliced too.

Now the voice was close to her ear.

"Every Reaper will die, gutted," it said. "In the meantime, enjoy your meals."

Petrov listened as slow, heavy footsteps padded away from her. Wildly, she clawed at the cloth knotted behind her head. When the chamois finally tore free, she saw a crescent moon directly above Shadow Canyon in the slate sky. She'd been unconscious for hours.

Across the creek, a monstrous silhouette glided through a dark stand of pygmy pines. It flung something upward with the same metallic *zing* she'd heard before. A hundred feet up, sparks spit off the cliff face.

Then the great fluttering shadow rose straight up the canyon wall and disappeared.

3

SKIRMISHER

DAROX GINGERLY TOUCHED the spot where they'd punctured his skull and torn out the implant.

Crosshatched with metal sutures, the crude incision over the occipital bone was still numb and oozing orange blood. He dabbed hemp oil on the swollen seam in his scalp, as instructed. He'd been fully conscious during the procedure.

Now he sat cross-legged on a woven mat in his hut, exploring the neural flow of unobstructed thought across his prefrontal cortex. He'd been meditating for two hours since the extraction. The Skirmisher celebration rite would begin shortly.

Outside, someone shook the hut's front flap.

"Come in," called Darox.

The flap folded inward and a tall, broad figure clad in onyx body armor ducked into the room. "Are you well?" he asked.

Darox nodded. They gazed at each other with large, silvery, pupilless eyes.

The other, named Mahnk, smiled slightly and asked, "Do you feel different?"

"Yes," said Darox. He hesitated. "Well. Somewhat."

They said the surgery would change him, and he did feel changed. But he expected more—a surge of emotion, perhaps, or revelation. He glanced over at the gray alloy chest plate hanging on his wall hook. Something about it seemed altered. Nothing was really different, not objectively. But he seemed to see it anew. It was odd. He watched Mahnk wrinkle the nasal slits of his flattened, snakelike nose.

"Can you smell the feast?" asked Mahnk.

"I can," replied Darox.

"Are you hungry?"

"No."

Mahnk sat on a low stool. "Did it hurt?"

"Some."

Mahnk's own extraction was scheduled for the following day. He nodded solemnly. "I do not mind pain when it's unexpected or sudden, such as in combat." He leaned forward, elbows resting on his knees. "But to sit in a chair and let someone drill into . . ." He stopped, looking up. His alien eyes darkened to a leaden gray. "While awake!"

Darox was amused. "When the chip is finally out . . . you know, they showed it to me," he said.

Mahnk frowned. "Your extraction?"

"Yes."

"Good god."

Darox nodded. "Trust me, when you see it, any pain you feel will become irrelevant."

For years—from his murky "birth" until just two hours ago—

Darox's occipital lobe had hosted a wireless neurochip. This chip received instructions transmitted psionically from a central ADVENT command center. These transmissions translated directly and instantaneously into both cognition and biomechanical impulses.

Nobody knew the location of the source, the so-called ADVENT Network Tower; some skeptics even suggested it was a propagandistic myth. But Darox did not doubt its existence. He had felt its centrality. He had seen troopers in coordinated maneuvers, given no verbal or visual commands, yet moving in perfect sync with his own irresistible and unconscious urges.

Darox could see that Mahnk was uneasy, so he said, "Tomorrow will be a good day for you, brother. Trust me."

"What does it look like?" asked Mahnk.

"The chip?"

"Yes!"

Darox shook his head. "I cannot tell you," he replied.

"Yes, you can," urged Mahnk.

"It would spoil the surprise."

Mahnk grunted and widened his eyes.

Amused again, Darox raised his thick brow. A cold chinook gust rattled the hut. They both looked up as the nanofiber ceiling undulated.

"Winter is coming," said Mahnk.

Darox nodded. "That means fewer alien patrols," he said. "Fewer convoys for resupply raids." With a sly grin, he added, "Fewer training opportunities."

Mahnk raised a fist. "So I say we go to the lowlands," he said.

"To the lowlands," nodded Darox.

Mahnk frowned thoughtfully. "How long, I wonder, before we can take the fight into the New Cities?"

"We need better psionics first," said Darox.

"True."

Darox grinned. "And we need to tear that chip out of your head," he said.

Mahnk looked ill.

* * *

Mahnk was the first fellow recruit Darox had met eight months earlier shortly after both were "liberated" (i.e., disabled by stun batons, then kidnapped). Skirmisher infiltration units had plucked them from separate ADVENT checkpoints outside New Seattle.

Since then, they'd been shuttled nearly thirteen hundred miles, moving tribe to tribe along the old Canadian border and then southeast down the Divide. They ended up at Wildcat, a Skirmisher reorientation center on the Mosquito Range near Leadville, Colorado. Then came six hard months of boot camp.

All Skirmishers, of course, were former ADVENT Troopers: hybrid clones, part human, part alien. But when liberated, new recruits had their neurochips immediately disabled with a pulsed radiofrequency ablation, an unpleasant, mind-scrambling experience. Suddenly cut off from the incessant flow of ADVENT's tactical command and control, Skirmisher recruits became disoriented and often useless in combat.

This called for extensive retraining.

Over time, most new Skirmishers responded well to liberation and what they called "freethinking." Rugged alpine training at eleven thousand feet in the high passes of Colorado's Western Slope also meshed well with the hybrid's physiology. ADVENT troops were genetically designed for hardship and spartan regimens.

When a recruit's retraining was complete, his neurochip was surgically removed in an initiation rite that included formal assignment to a Skirmisher tribe. If, like Darox, the recruit had also come from ADVENT's officer corps, he might be designated a tactical combat commander as well.

* * *

Looking at Mahnk, Darox suddenly understood something about his new reality.

"While meditating, I had a thought," he said. "It was an image, actually. Very vivid."

"What did you see?" asked Mahnk.

"I saw myself in battle," said Darox.

Mahnk's eyes brightened. "Excellent!" he said.

Darox tapped his chest. "But I was fighting for ADVENT again," he said. "Moving down the street of a shantytown, hunting rebels. I commanded a squad . . . but oddly, I was alone. As in those old days, the mission orders were my only thoughts. I was utterly alone with these thoughts."

Mahnk nodded solemnly. "That feeling is familiar," he said.

"I felt alien," said Darox. "Or, more accurately, I felt the alien blood in me. I felt as the purebred alien must feel."

Mahnk closed his eyes. "I have that memory too. It is always very cold."

Darox smiled. "But then the image changed," he said. "I saw myself advancing through woods with my Skirmisher brothers— you and the others." He pointed ahead of him. "Our mission was similar, but my thoughts were different."

"How so, brother?"

"The mission was important," said Darox. "But my thoughts were with my team. Our mutual survival was paramount. Our tactics reflected that. We pushed ahead but always in support positions. Always watching each other's back."

Mahnk nodded again. "True," he said. "It is the Skirmisher way."

"It is the *human* way," replied Darox. "This is the imperative of our human blood. Our feelings are stronger for each other than for the mission." Another strong gust of wind rattled the hut. After a long silence, Mahnk turned up his palms. "Before we go . . . please, tell me what they're going to pull out of my brain tomorrow."

Darox grinned and slowly uncrossed his legs. "It looks like a crystal spider."

Mahnk leaned back and blinked several times in horror.

"What?!"

"A spider," repeated Darox. He held out his hand and wiggled his fingers.

Mahnk looked ill.

"Or maybe a jellyfish," said Darox. He held his thumb and forefinger about a centimeter apart. "A small translucent capsule, this big, with long, threadlike tendrils." His eyes narrowed. "I am told some of these extend well into the frontal lobe. Fortunately, they slide right out."

Mahnk stood up. He flipped open the tent flap.

"I am going to be sick," he said.

Darox laughed, rose up himself, and clapped Mahnk on the back. As a former officer, he stood nearly six-and-a-half feet tall, a few inches taller than his compatriot.

He said, "No, brother, you're going to be free."

* * *

Skirmisher culture was a curiosity.

Its clan structure and tribal customs seemed to be rooted in deep wells of tradition, the product of generations of cultural evolution. An outsider might find it hard to believe, then, that the very first Skirmisher, Betos, not only was still breathing but also had founded the faction just two decades earlier. Even more curious: There wasn't a Skirmisher alive who was more than twenty years old.

The reason: Skirmishers were initially ADVENT Troopers "born" as mature warriors in top secret alien cloning labs. Strict chronology in years did not apply to their physical or mental development—not in a human sense, anyway. Darox, for example, was just eleven years old. Mahnk was eight.

Nobody knew where these ADVENT birthing labs were located. And nobody knew the exact process; no Skirmisher retained that memory. But creation theories abounded. Some said ADVENT Troopers were built "from scratch," emerging from a vat of DNA soup as identical clones, then genetically treated to create a narrow range of physical types. Others said troopers started as human "volunteers" who were mind-wiped, submerged in a bio-tank, and then subjected to alien DNA grafts. In this version, the process was said to trigger a gruesome and excruciating cell-by-cell transformation that took weeks to complete.

Whatever the case, given how recently they'd been cracking heads as brutal ADVENT "peacekeepers," Skirmisher initiates had to clear a high bar of trust, even within their own tribes. For the same reason, other Resistance cells regarded the entire Skirmisher faction with deep suspicion, even hostility.

As a result, Skirmishers kept to themselves.

They planned and executed anti-alien operations independent of other rebel groups. They stuck to the Wild Lands, scattering across the continent in nomadic, highly mobile clans. Over twenty years, their culture had grown increasingly insular, with unique and sometimes eccentric subcultures emerging from tribe to tribe.

But one Skirmisher practice that never changed was the initiation rite.

* * *

Kneeling on a cushion, teeth gritted tightly in pain, Darox leaned forward, resting his head on a low padded podium. Two Skirmisher artists bent over him, jabbing at the back of his scalp with sterilized tattoo needles.

The swollen flesh bordering his surgical lesion formed the barn-red back of a falcon—specifically, an American kestrel, the great ambush hunter of the high country. Vivid blue-gray wings spread on either side, wrapping the back of Darox's skull. This was the tribal marking of the Kestrel clan of Skirmishers.

Other than a small cadre of sentries posted out thirty miles in each direction, the entire Wildcat camp, including the reorientation staff and all initiates, attended the marking rite.

As the artists added the final touches, a powerful, imposing figure in jet-black body armor rose from a camping stool. A red Ute-style ceremonial robe draped his massive shoulders. When the artists finished, he stepped in front of Darox and raised his hand.

"Rise, brother," he said.

Darox lifted his head, wincing at the new pain on the back of his scalp. Still kneeling, he stared up at the face above him.

"Do you know me?" asked the robed figure.

"Yes," said Darox, bowing his head.

Every Skirmisher knew Mox. Once a much-feared ADVENT captain, he was now the right hand of the first-liberated Betos, founder of the Skirmisher clan. Darox had met Mox once before. The great leader had briefly inspected the newly liberated recruits outside New Seattle. Darox had been manacled in a cage then.

"Are we kin?" asked Mox.

"Every Skirmisher is kin," said Darox, a mantra he'd heard at camp after camp a thousand times.

"Then do not bow to me," said Mox.

Darox quickly raised his head. He looked up at Mox, whose eyes had darkened. The great leader folded his massive arms.

"I will say it again," said Mox. "Rise."

Now Darox stood.

Mox leaned forward and said, "Never kneel again." He jabbed at his own chest. "You are different inside. Do you understand?"

"Yes."

"Good." Mox stepped back and studied Darox. "I have heard about your close combat skills. Your trainers are quite impressed."

Darox raised his brow but said nothing. His Wildcat trainers were some of the fiercest and finest soldiers he'd ever seen. Far better than even the elite ADVENT officers he'd seen terrorize Resistance pockets in the townships ringing New Seattle.

Abruptly, Mox turned toward a pair of warriors, one male and one female, standing separate from the surrounding audience. They bore the same American kestrel markings across the back of their skulls.

"These are your tribe," said Mox. "Tomorrow they will escort you up-country to your new home, where the others are preparing for the arrival of their new tactical officer."

Darox raised his brow again. "Officer?"

Mox smiled slightly. "You have considerable command experience," he said.

"But only as ADVENT. I am not qualified to . . ."

Mox cut him off. "You will report to Tashl, your tribal chief. You will oversee all combat operations from the high camp."

Darox knew the Kestrel were currently encamped in the Holy Cross Wilderness ten miles away and another three thousand feet higher than the Wildcat settlement. Like most Skirmisher tribes, they kept their community on the move; all base camps relocated every three to four weeks. He turned to face the two tribesmen. Fists clenched, each of them crossed both arms across their chest—the Skirmisher salute. Darox saluted in return.

Suddenly, Mox's adjutant Loka burst from the command hut, waving a PDA tablet. She approached Mox.

"Shawnee Peak just went code orange," she said. He held up the tablet. "We have ADVENT transports inbound from New Denver."

"How many?"

"Five."

Mox gestured to the sky. "Are they in standard search spread?"

Darox knew that an ADVENT squadron's flight formation told you a lot about their intentions. Loka tapped something into the keypad. After a few seconds, she said, "They are in attack delta, sir. And moving fast." The PDA beeped twice. "Ah, Mount Sherman spotters are now confirming approach."

"What vector?"

The adjutant pointed down at the ground in front of Mox.

Mox stared at her. "*Here?*"

"Yes, sir," she said. "Dead on."

Mox abruptly spun to the assembly. "Break down the huts," he ordered. "You have four minutes."

As Darox stepped toward his hut, Mox held out his hand to stop him.

"You," he said. "Pick a recon partner and come with me."

4

ASSASSIN

YEARS OF HOSTILE RELATIONS with parties in all directions had taught Skirmisher tribes the value of "rapid decamp." Even large-scale settlements like Wildcat could disappear in less time than an ADVENT Troop Transport could fly from a horizon sighting to ground zero.

But this was the first time Darox had actually seen the drill live: an entire hut-village disassembled, shuttled into a dry-wash ravine, and stashed under sheets of camouflaged canvas. In fewer than five minutes, the two-acre site along old Highway 9 above Turquoise Lake reverted to a nondescript mountain meadow.

Meanwhile, Mox and a team of six Wildcat trainers grabbed their gear. Darox was already in full battle dress for the ceremony, but he ducked inside his hut to snag his Kal-7 Bullpup shotgun before the camp crew could pack it up. As he emerged, weapon in hand, he spotted Mahnk hauling a gear bag to the tree line.

Darox whistled loudly and ran to him.

"Exciting, eh?" said Mahnk.

"Very."

"Five transports!" said Mahnk with relish. "You will spill much orange blood today, brother."

"No," said Darox, grinning. "We will."

Mahnk stared. "What?"

Darox nodded toward Mox, who was fastening his armor. "Our leader wants a recon team." He kicked the gear bag out of Mahnk's hand. "Let's go." As another recruit ran past, Darox directed him to grab the bag.

Mahnk laughed loudly. "I am speechless!"

"Good," said Darox.

They joined the full tactical team at the edge of the clearing. Then Mox led them up a steep slope into a thick stand of pines. Just twenty yards into the trees they hit a devil's den of overgrown boulders, the bottom of an ancient rockslide.

Darox and Mahnk exchanged a look. They knew this spot well. They'd trained in it for many hours.

"We lure them here," called Mox. He pointed to a huge toppled tree trunk to the right of the rock spill. "Recon, after you engage, fall back there." He gave Darox a look. "You will be our flank."

Darox nodded.

Skirmishers were good fighters at any range. But up close, they were particularly lethal. Compact, hard-hitting shotguns combined with retractable Ripjack razor claws integrated into every Skirmisher's armored gauntlet. Wildcat trainers had spent countless hours drilling Darox, Mahnk, and the other recruits on the finer points of close quarters combat in tight, complicated spaces.

This jumble of boulders was perfect.

Darox turned and pushed back through the trees to the top of the slope they'd climbed. Recon's role was to mark enemy numbers, then lure them into the kill zone. Mahnk took up a position a few yards down the tree line.

Three howling ADVENT Troop Transports hovered over the meadow below them, the same meadow where a full forty-hut village had bustled just moments before. The other two transports banked hard left, following the cracked asphalt of Highway 9.

"Familiar sight, isn't it?" crackled Mahnk.

Darox touched the earpiece of his headset.

"Three birds landing," he reported. "Two more bearing west."

In his earpiece, Mox bellowed, "Hotel, you got that?"

Now Darox's earpiece crackled with the voice of the adjutant, Loka. "Acknowledged," she replied. "I am patching in the Skinner Hut garrison."

"This is Skinner Hut," crackled another voice.

"Two ATTs bearing your way," reported the adjutant. "Are you ready up there?"

"I would say we are eager."

Darox heard Mox chuckle over the line.

* * *

Each hulking ADVENT Transport was battleship gray with red light strips highlighting the extended wings. The engine whine was so familiar that Darox actually relaxed a bit; in his ADVENT days, he'd listened hard for that very sound while nervously awaiting evacuation from unfriendly slums and shantytowns.

As each ship neared the ground, its wings flipped up to landing position, revealing a side exit hatch. Each hatch hissed loudly, then slid open to reveal a standard ADVENT peacekeeper squad: one red-helmet officer with a trio of gray-armor troopers. But as these hybrid soldiers hopped from their transports, a Chryssalid suddenly burrowed out of the ground nearby and skittered behind each squad.

"Bugs," said Mahnk in disgust.

"Marking three Chryssalids," reported Darox.

In his earpiece, he heard Mox murmur, "Interesting."

Over the radio, Loka said, "We have not seen bugs up here in ten years."

During his days in ADVENT operations, Darox had often deployed with alien support units. All of them seemed menacing, but the Chryssalids were the worst. He'd never felt safe with the spiky, slavering monsters on the hunt nearby. Their indiscriminate attacks on innocent civilians had a grisly ferocity. Sometimes they seemed out of control. He'd half expected to get a claw in the back himself.

Now the bugs were the enemy. He found the prospect both chilling and satisfying.

As the ADVENT transports lifted off to hover out of range in overwatch positions, the ground troops began their scan of the meadow. Several units clustered to inspect the circle of flattened grass where the Wildcat command hut had stood. Darox unclipped a frag grenade from his vest and let it fly. The explosion took out two troopers and severely mangled one of the Chryssalids.

"Well tossed!" shouted Mahnk with glee as he opened fire with his shotgun.

Their concentrated fire took out one of the ADVENT officers, another trooper, and the wounded bug. But once the nearest officers marked their positions, the return mag-rifle fire got hot fast. Darox and Mahnk withdrew through the trees to the rockslide and took cover behind the fallen trunk as Mox had ordered.

* * *

ADVENT Troopers were conceived as urban shock troops, trained primarily as riot-control police. Their gear and tactics were suited to the orderly geometry of the New Cities, not the wild tangle of alpine forests. The units that rushed aggressively up the slope and into the trees seemed woefully unprepared for the Skirmisher ambush that awaited them.

Both remaining ADVENT officers fell in the first Kal-7 salvo from Mox and his Wildcat team. The suddenly leaderless troopers scattered into the rocky den, taking up largely indefensible positions that were easily flanked. Only the two remaining Chryssalids moved with any sort of tactical intelligence. But another frag grenade flushed one insectoid out of cover into shotgun range; the other bug died trying to burrow behind a boulder, unaware that two Skirmisher warriors hunkered in an open rock chimney just behind it.

The battle lasted mere minutes, and it was a thing of beauty to watch. Darox and Mahnk didn't have to fire a single shot, much less defend the flank. They marveled as Mox and the Wildcat crew shattered the hapless assault quickly and efficiently. One of the trainers even managed to flank and stun two enemy troopers, then jam PRF electrode needles into the backs of their heads to ablate the neurochips. If they survived this crude field procedure, the troopers would soon become new Skirmisher recruits.

Mahnk stepped out of cover. "That was certainly invigorating!" he said.

"Impressive," agreed Darox.

Voices crackled in his earpiece. From the sound of it, the other two ADVENT transports that veered west up the Glacier Creek route had fared even worse than their mates. Skirmishers based at Skinner Hut, part of the old Tenth Mountain Division network of shelters, caught the ADVENT and their Chryssalids in a nasty crossfire between the cliff walls in nearby Hagerman Pass.

"I believe the human term for this is a 'turkey shoot,'" reported the Skinner Hut squad leader over the radio.

"Survivors?" asked Mox.

"None, sir, unfortunately. No recruits."

Mox's adjutant, Loka, broke into the frequency. "All five transports just hightailed home," she reported.

Hearing this, Mahnk grunted and looked at Darox. "How does ADVENT know so fast?"

"Psionics," said Darox. He tapped the back of his head. "Brain chip goes cold, the Network Tower instantly knows you are dead."

"And then they just fly away," said Mahnk in disgust, arcing his hand through the air. "Leaving you behind like a piece of garbage tossed out the hatch." He stared angrily at one of the Chryssalid corpses. "Almost makes me feel bad for this abomination."

"I hope it died in agony, feeling alone and betrayed," said Darox.

Mahnk slowly smiled. "You hate bugs," he said.

"I hate aliens."

"But you are half alien."

"I hate that half."

Mahnk guffawed. "Me too, brother!"

* * *

The team began stripping the enemy dead of their ammo, equipment, and other items. As usual, they found no intel: no maps, orders, field reports, nothing. ADVENT troops never carried such items, not even the officers. All strategic directives came psionically from ADVENT central command.

Mox suddenly burst through a pine shrub stand.

"Leave it!" he called.

Something about his tone made Darox look up. Mox was staring at him, darkly.

"Darox," he said. His voice was tense.

"Yes, sir?"

Mox motioned him over. Then the Skirmisher leader led him through a gulley to a barely visible trailhead off the old highway.

Waiting there were the two Kestrel clan members he'd seen at the ceremony. Mox introduced them: Koros and Rika. Both looked grim and edgy.

"Our camp has gone silent," said Rika.

"Radio silence?" asked Darox.

Rika shook her head. "Total silence," she said. "They are not responding to anything."

Koros said, "Not even tap code."

Skirmisher sites often went radio silent when ADVENT patrols with high psionics were in the area. Instead of radio chatter, they relied on a simple code of mike tapping that could be disguised as the popping of random radio static.

Mox pointed north up the pass.

"Go now," he said. "Keep the channel open. I will have a support team ready."

Darox reached over his shoulder and yanked his shotgun from his back-sling. Checking its autoload magazine, he said, "I would like to take my recon partner too."

Mox narrowed his silver eyes. "What is his name again?"

"Mahnk," said Darox. "His chip extraction is scheduled for tomorrow."

Mox nodded. "I suppose he would like to be a Kestrel too," he said. "Is that possible?"

Mox just headed back toward the gulley. "I will send him out."

As Mox disappeared, Darox turned to the others. Both looked at him quizzically. He said, "Mahnk fights hard, and he is a good brother."

Koros rubbed his cheek. "But is he fast?"

"Fast enough."

"Good," said Rika. He could see that she struggled to maintain calm. "We have ten hard miles ahead of us, and we will not wait for him if he lags."

Darox nodded. "Mahnk will keep up."

"And what about you?" she asked sharply.

Darox nearly responded with equal sting, but then he saw it in her eyes: Her clan was up there, and they weren't answering calls.

"You will not lose me," he said.

* * *

The hike up into the Holy Cross Wilderness was difficult and at times treacherous. But it was stunningly beautiful. As they traversed a granite shelf in Fall Creek Pass to bypass a collapsed switchback trail, Darox gazed out at the postcard vista of wildflower meadows rolling toward Lake Constantine.

He thought, Another ADVENT lie.

In his ADVENT days, Darox had seen the propaganda videos depicting all Wild Lands as devastated, polluted, toxic, and dangerous. But this was pristine country. No sign of the firestorms that had charred the Front Range. Looking back south, he could see the humped snowcap of Mount Massive, second highest peak in the North American Rockies. It was twenty miles away, but it seemed he could reach out and touch it.

Glancing over at Mahnk, he said, "I feel nothing but awe up here."

Mahnk clung to an outcrop. Kicking for a foothold, he gasped, "Yes, if only one could breathe."

Darox inhaled deep. "The air is thin," he agreed. "But clean, brother."

Grunting, Mahnk swung onto the ledge where Darox stood. He said, "Twelve thousand feet . . . is far too many feet."

Ahead, Rika and Koros scrambled lightly over a saddle in the ridge and disappeared. Neither had spoken for hours as they pressed ahead urgently, no breaks, eating and drinking on the move. But when Darox crossed the saddle too, he found them crouched in a ravine next to a swirling creek, waiting. Up ahead, water cascaded downhill over a series of boulders and rock steps.

Koros pointed to the top.

"Tuhare Lake is up there," he said quietly. "Those are its outlet falls."

Rika gazed grimly up the chute. She said, "The camp is by the feeder stream on the far shore. Or, it was when we left."

Darox crouched next to her. "Why would ADVENT come way up here?" he asked.

She gave him a fierce look. "I do not know."

"It makes no sense."

Koros dipped his green bandana in the creek, wiped his face, and said, "ADVENT would not come here. They have no alpine training."

Darox said, "Exactly."

"There was a code orange alert," said Koros. "Maybe Tashl simply took precautions and decamped to one of the sanctuary caves."

Rika gave him a fierce look. "But why total silence?" she said.

Koros shrugged. "Let's go see," he said.

Darox stood and pulled out his shotgun.

"I will take point," he said.

When Rika tried to protest, Koros put his big gloved hand on her arm. "Today," he said, "he is your tactical commander."

Mahnk stood up. "And tomorrow as well," he growled.

Koros nodded. "Of course."

Darox led the way up the steep, twisting trail that rose beside the falls. At the top, they took cover behind a long granite slab. Ahead, Tuhare Lake glittered blue on the treeless alpine terrace, filling a great cirque carved from the ridge. A rock-strewn meadow of yellowing grasses and scrub circled one side; a crumbling cliff face walled off the other side.

On the far shore two hundred meters away sat a small cluster of Skirmisher huts.

Mahnk quickly pulled a scope from his utility pouch and put it to his eye. "Looks undisturbed," he said.

"Any movement?" asked Darox.

"None. I see no one."

Rika pointed and said, "The only approach is through the open meadow there."

"Cover me," said Darox.

He scrambled from rock to rock through the tall grasses. When he reached a gulley on the far shore, he waved for the others, who followed one at a time. Then Darox led the way up a gentle slope to the camp perimeter.

Both Koros and Rika glanced around, frowning. Nothing stirred. Each of the small, low-slung personal huts had the Kestrel marking over the entry flap. Darox stepped into the nearest one. Its sparse interior was nearly identical to his own back at Wildcat and to every other Skirmisher hut he'd entered over the past months. Inside: two sleeping pallets, two canvas storage pouches, a collapsible solar stove.

The weapon and armor hooks on the wall were empty.

"They left with their combat gear," said Darox.

Mahnk nodded, glancing around. "Ready to fight," he said.

Outside, they heard Koros howl.

* * *

He knelt at the entry hatch to the large communal hut used for tribal meals and meetings. Rika sat next to him.

"What is this?" he cried out.

An image had been flash-seared into the Mylar shroud on the exterior wall. It was the silhouette profile of a towering, alien-looking figure—monstrous, open-mouthed, fangs bared, armed with twin swords. Smaller figures surrounded it, slain and falling.

Etched under the image was an ADVENT language phrase that translated to:

YOU BETRAY YOUR OWN CREATION

Darox raised his shotgun and kicked open the hut door to find his tribe.

* * *

All twelve kills were precise and clean.

All suffered deep blade cuts.

All twelve seemed to have fallen with little, if any, struggle.

The bodies were arranged like spokes in a wheel, feet out, heads touching at the hub.

The forehead of each Kestrel corpse was stamped with the ADVENT word for "Traitor" in corrosive ink.

On the wall, written in orange hybrid blood, was another ADVENT phrase that translated to this:

I AM THE ASSASSIN

5

AVENGER

THE BARTENDER HAD the bottle uncorked before Dr. Marin even reached the barstool. The scientist smiled ruefully.

"Thanks, Danny," he said.

Danny poured the club soda into a tall glass of ice. "Make it a double, doc?"

"Sure," said Marin. "You only live once."

He watched Danny fill the glass to the brim, then add a squeeze of lime.

"Straw?" asked Danny.

"Hell no."

Danny slid the glass forward. He said, "It's not true, you know."

"What's not?" asked Marin, sipping the soda.

"Living only once."

Marin sighed.

"What, you don't believe in heaven?" asked Danny.

"I'm a scientist, man. I believe in particles."

"Particles?"

"Right," said Marin. He clumped his hands together and then threw them apart. "See? They aggregate, they disaggregate."

"Yeah?" Danny recorked the soda bottle. "So how do they aggregate into, like, a pony?"

"Gremlins," said Marin.

Danny snorted a laugh. But then he got serious and said, "Doc, I'm telling you, I'm on my second life. And don't worry, it ain't religious."

Marin nodded. "Is this a story?"

"Possibly."

"Bartenders are supposed to listen to stories, not tell them."

"Right. Do you have a story?"

Marin rubbed his cheek, thinking. Then: "No."

"Then shut up and listen."

Amused, Marin said, "Okay. Pour yourself a club soda and put it on my tab."

* * *

His full name was Dr. William Pendleton Marin III.

The Pendleton came from his mother's side, an obscenely wealthy and politically powerful family in Nebraska until the aliens plasma-bombed Omaha, triggering a holocaust that rivaled the Dresden inferno of World War II.

In 2014, the year the invasion fleet arrived, Marin was fresh out of UC Berkeley with a newly minted PhD in human evolutionary biology. He'd just started postdoctoral work at Harvard when the first extraterrestrial pods hit Vancouver, Beijing, Chicago, and a number of other major cities worldwide.

Academic research collapsed as the incursions spread and became increasingly horrific over the following months. Marin was about to return home to the family compound in Omaha when his old mentor from Berkeley, Dr. Parag Bhandari, called and urged him to interview with an odd, eccentric woman in Washington, DC.

Her name was Dr. Moira Vahlen, and she hired Marin into her XCOM science lab.

The appointment gave him a great sense of purpose. It also saved his life. The Pendleton family compound—and most of the Pendleton family—fell victim to the gruesome incendiary attack that basically melted an entire Midwestern American city off the map.

"So I'm on patrol up in Greenland, and this guy shoots me in the face," said Danny.

Marin laughed. "Great start," he said.

"It gets better." Danny leaned his forearms on the bar. "Sure you don't want a little whiskey in that soda, doc?"

Marin held up a hand. "Sober seventeen years."

"I got the good stuff here, man."

"Last time I drank . . ." Marin paused, looking at his glass. "It's a bad story. I'd rather hear yours."

Danny nodded. "Okay," he said.

"So you're in Greenland."

"Freezing my ass off," said Danny. "Because I'm walking on the largest ice sheet in the world. Did you know that Greenland is, like, seven hundred thousand square miles of ice?"

"I did, actually."

Danny just stared at him. "Of course you did."

"Sorry. I'm a huge nerd."

"Well, I didn't know it was all ice. I thought it would be, you know, green up there."

"Iceland is green," said Marin. "Greenland is ice."

"See? If I'd paid attention at school, I'd know that. And I wouldn't be stuck here tending bar."

Danny Roman, of course, was much more than just a bartender. He was an XCOM lieutenant, Grenadier class, one of the best heavy weapons specialists in the agency. A number of the Avenger-based soldiers took turns tending the ship's bar in off-hours. It was a great way to decompress after deploying on yet another tense covert operation, the only kind of operations XCOM engaged in now in its role as a hunted, heavily outnumbered, underground resistance force.

As Danny continued his story, Marin glanced over at the glass display case next to the bar. On the top shelf sat a framed photo of XCOM's original "A" team. In the center stood Dr. Vahlen in her white lab coat. As XCOM's chief scientist, she'd pioneered the study of psionics, Marin's current area of expertise.

On her right stood the late Dr. Raymond Shen, XCOM's legendary first chief engineer. To her left stood a considerably younger-looking version of Central Officer John Bradford, the only one of the three here now aboard XCOM's new Avenger base. Referred to simply as "Central" by everyone in the agency, Bradford now sported a nasty facial scar, along with a darker, more cynical take on things.

* * *

Half an hour later, Dr. Marin was wrapping up a game of Chicken Foot with two guys from Chief Lily Shen's engineering lab. As he slid two dominoes into place, he said, "It's looking good for me, boys."

"Not fair," said one of the engineers, a stout, bearded fellow named Jack Maples. "You're using science to cheat."

"How?"

Maples shrugged. "How would I know? I'm just an engineer. I deal in real-world applications, so I'm incapable of cheating or even understanding the concept of cheating."

Marin grinned. "How are things down in your lab?"

The other guy, Kenji Kojima, tapped his lone remaining domino. "Doing good on plasma," he said. "Not so good on the new alien biotech."

"Really?" said Marin. "The science was such a straight line."

Kojima shrugged. Then he said, "What's up with PERG?"

The Psionic Energy Research Group (PERG) was Marin's lab. Like the mobile Avenger base that housed it, PERG had come a long way in a very short time. Since the massive alien supply vessel was discovered at a jungle crash site in the shadow of India's Western Ghats, the Avenger had been secured (at great cost); overhauled with front-edge stealth absorption and refractive index technologies, reducing its airborne spectral signature to that of a large crow; then retrofitted and transformed into XCOM's flying operations center. The Avenger and its small Skyranger fleet—by then XCOM had recovered and refurbished three of the old troop transports—were virtually invisible in terms of both optical and electromagnetic wavelengths.

In like manner, PERG had grown from a single dedicated scientist—Dr. Marin—to a small team of experts from around the globe. The group's research proceeded along two basic lines of inquiry: detection and latency. Latency research was based on XCOM's old GEIST Program; it focused on tapping latent psionic sensitivity in human subjects. Detection research sought to develop tools that could find, trace, measure, and even tap into psionic sources out in the field.

As head of PERG, Marin oversaw both efforts, but his hands-on work was with the detection team. Resources were limited, so PERG's psionic sensor grid was limited to North America and had many holes in coverage. But the group had been tracking a growing scatterplot of psionic anomalies for months—strange hot spots, sprouting up far from the New Cities where alien psionic power was concentrated.

"We're getting really high-activity readings in some odd places," said Marin, studying the domino layout on the bar.

"Define odd," said Maples.

"Like, out in the middle of east jesus nowhere," replied Marin.

"So ADVENT is pushing out into the hinterlands?" asked Maples.

Marin shook his head. "We cross-check everything with the military intel guys," he said. "None of the hot spots correlate to ADVENT troop movements or to any alien activity. These are weird psionic wells. They suddenly bubble up in places where no one goes."

"Like where?" asked Kojima.

"The first odd pings were way north in the Canadian Rockies," said Marin, "Then they started moving south. We picked up blooms in Wyoming and Colorado the last few months all up in the backcountry, crazy high elevations." He slid a domino into place. "Chickie fours."

Maples slapped his forehead. "You just shattered my play," he said.

"I bet it was a good one, Jack."

Maples sighed. "I hate scientists."

Kojima kept tapping his only domino. "You want to drop more sensor pods up there in the Rockies, Will?" he asked.

Marin cocked his head. "Well, I know you're strapped," he said.

"Right," said Kojima. "But this sounds promising."

Marin smiled. Kenji Kojima had always been a good partner with the science division. Some of the engineering team had a turf war mentality, always scrapping and competing for the meager resources available to the Avenger labs. But Kojima appreciated good science, and he had the chief engineer's ear. Thanks to him, Lily Shen had offered generous help in the past.

"Thanks, Kenji," said Marin. "I'll let you know."

Lieutenant Roman stepped out of a small inventory closet behind the bar.

"I've taken stock, gentlemen," he announced. He took a deep breath. "It's not good in there."

Maples frowned at his empty whiskey tumbler. "Danny, can we fly to Scotland and restock?" he asked. "Like, right now?"

"Sure, Jack," said Danny. "I'll let Central know. He's a connoisseur of the Highland single malts."

Suddenly, a voice blared over the ship's intercom:

Dr. William Marin, please report to the Research Division immediately. Dr. Marin, report to Research immediately.

Kojima raised his eyebrows. "That sounds urgent," he said.

"It does," said Marin, standing. He pulled a cell-comm out of his pocket. "Ah, no wonder they're paging me. I turned it off."

Danny grabbed Marin's empty soda glass and waggled it. "Sure you can drive, doc?"

Marin grinned. "I'll call a taxi."

* * *

The XCOM Research Lab wrapped around the Avenger's pulsing power core. It was surprisingly airy for a shipboard facility—in fact, half its space was still undeveloped. As the lab's security doors whooshed open, Marin rushed inside and nearly ran into Dr. Richard Tygan, XCOM's new chief scientist.

"Ah, Will," said Dr. Tygan, nodding.

"Hello, Richard," replied Marin.

"Your team seems very excited," said Tygan. "Maybe you can brief me after you meet. I'll be over in the autopsy bay."

"Sure thing," said Marin. "Who are you cutting up today? Anybody I know?"

Tygan grinned. "We're just running a pathology report on tissue samples from that new Muton breed."

"Ah," said Marin. "That explains the smell."

Tygan grimaced. "Yes," he said. "I'd heard about the famous aroma, but this is my first one."

Dr. Tygan was a true outsider; he not only had no history with XCOM but also came directly from a stint in ADVENT's infamous gene therapy clinics. But Tygan's preinvasion resume at both the University of Chicago and Trident Pharmaceuticals was stellar. He was well-known in the scientific community for groundbreaking research in immunosuppressant drugs used for organ transplant procedures. Like many respected research scientists, he'd had no choice but to take work offered by the ADVENT government.

"So we finally scored a new Muton for autopsy?" asked Marin.

"Sadly, no," replied Tygan. "One of our Rangers sliced off a Muton fillet during a scrum with one of the monsters. Good DNA sample."

Marin winced. "How's our guy doing?"

"The Muton clobbered him good, but he's alive." Dr. Tygan waved him on. "Hurry," he said. "Your people are jumping around over there."

"Any idea what it is?" asked Marin as he turned toward the lab's psionics alcove.

"I was hoping they found Dr. Vahlen," said Tygan.

"Ha!" said Marin. "My guess is Moira won't be 'found' until she wants to be."

Tygan nodded. "I'd love to meet her," he said. He smiled slyly. "She could be the boss, and I could get back to my petri dishes."

Marin laughed. "You'd like her, Richard," he said.

"I bet I would."

Months earlier, back before the Avenger had been found, Dr. Vahlen had barely dodged a brutal ADVENT ambush of XCOM's secret Wunderland research facility in Antarctica. After she escaped, she went dark. Once it became clear that Vahlen was staying off the grid, the Shens had approached Dr. Marin about stepping into her role as chief scientist. But he'd respectfully declined. He knew his limitations; he wasn't a visionary like Vahlen, and he couldn't juggle the roles of wily administrator and uncompromising advocate like she'd so expertly done. He was pleased when XCOM recruited Tygan for the job. So far, so good.

Marin did, however, retain the job of managing the psionics group. The work was intense, riveting, and critically important. And his people were a great bunch. Young, smart, oddball. It was a job that he relished every day.

"What's up?" he asked as he approached a long console studded with multicolored LED lights and digital readouts.

A shaggy-haired young tech named Jared Gilmore stood on a chair, gazing up at the huge monitor above the console. The screen was blank. He was just twenty-eight, but his work had already taken the global detection grid to an entirely new level.

"What are you doing, Gilmore?" asked Marin. He turned to another member of the team, thirty-year-old Bonnie Lopez, sitting at the console with her hands hovering over the touchscreen controls. Purple hair draped from her baseball cap. "Lopez, what's he doing?"

Still staring at the screen, Gilmore pointed down at Lopez.

"Okay, sis, let's tap NavSat 36 for the CX-10 video," he said. "Now!"

Lopez clicked a control button. An old-fashioned hourglass icon started filling on-screen, marking the time to connection.

Dr. Marin's eyes widened with alarm. "Video?" he said. "That's a lot of bandwidth." He frowned at Gilmore. "This better be good, buddy."

"Oh, it's good, boss," said Gilmore, his teeth flashing big.

NavSat 36 was one of several hundred geostationary satellites that served as conduits for ADVENT's global psionic network. Insanely massive amounts of alien data bounced off this orbital web every nanosecond; XCOM had learned it could tap into the stream in short intervals without getting detected.

The PERG team used this method regularly to monitor Gilmore's field sensors. Each sensor pod included instruments to detect and measure psionic energy readings plus a digital minicam for surveillance footage if a strong signal manifested.

On-screen, the words "SENSOR UPLOAD ROUTING: NavSat 36" appeared in a window. After just thirty seconds, it ended.

"Okay, out," said Gilmore.

Lopez tapped the touch control and the connection window disappeared.

Gilmore grinned at Dr. Marin. "Dude, things are popping," he said.

"You picked up another psionic bubble?"

"Bubble?" Gilmore cackled like a witch and looked at Lopez.

Lopez swiveled her chair to face Marin. "What do you drink, boss?" she asked.

Marin squinted. "Club soda?"

"Right." Lopez raised the brim of her cap. "It was like an entire glass of that stuff."

"That's . . . a lot of bubbles."

Gilmore hopped off the chair with a dramatic landing.

"The most bubbles ever," he said. He held his arms out wide.

Now Lopez started typing madly on the touchscreen. She glanced up at Gilmore and said, "While these video files are compiling, let's show Will what we just saw." Two satellite map images popped open in windows on the big screen.

"We got two good bursts in sequence," said Gilmore. "These recordings are at five-minute intervals, both triggered by the same sensor, CX-10." He pointed at the left image. "Check this out."

Lopez tapped a button, and the map image came alive. Clouds drifted over a rugged landscape.

"Where is this?" asked Marin, watching.

"Colorado," said Lopez. "We dropped this pod on Vail Pass. Way up high."

"Now add the filter, Bonnie," said Gilmore, rubbing his hands together briskly.

Lopez punched up an overlay designed to highlight psionic activity. After a few seconds, a bright purple dot pulsed on-screen. Then two more next to it. After a few seconds, a cluster of about two dozen dots started flashing nearby.

"Holy mother of god," said Marin.

The purple dots pulsed rapidly. Then the feed ended.

"Okay, now here's the second one," said Lopez, tapping another button. "Just five minutes later."

With the filter added to the second map image, the cluster of purple dots appeared to have fanned out in a circle around the first three dots. The furious pulsing continued.

Marin stepped closer to the screen. "What the hell is going on down there?" he said. "Can you zoom in closer from overhead?"

Lopez shook her head. "Unfortunately, no," she replied. "But given the location and high activity, I'm betting we have ground-level video of the event."

"Whatever it is," added Gilmore, eyes gleaming.

Marin stared at the maps, thinking. "Those wouldn't be ADVENT troops," he said. "Not way up there. They rarely send their grunts out into the Wild Lands, much less high-value psionic units."

"It's too *wild* out here," whispered Gilmore, grinning.

"Exactly."

Just then the console beeped.

"Video's ready," said Lopez.

As she tapped controls, Gilmore said, "We pulled two ninety-second clips that match up with the map sequences you just saw." He glanced at Lopez. "Bonnie, can you mark the sensor pod location on the maps first?"

"Gotcha," she replied. Up on both map windows, a red dot appeared.

Gilmore pointed up at it. "We dropped it on a ridgetop overlooking the old I-70 rest area, so it has a pretty wide-angle view of Vail Pass below."

Two video windows opened on-screen. Lopez clicked the first one open.

Dr. Marin frowned. "That's elk," he said.

Sure enough, a small elk herd lumbered across the old freeway. The sensor's minicam, programmed to track and zoom in on movement, followed the animals across the lanes.

"Psionic elk?" muttered Gilmore.

But within seconds, the elk plunged into trees on the road's far side; the camera view swung rapidly left while pulling back into a wider shot. A pair of ADVENT Troop Transports were landing on the roadway. Squads of ADVENT Troopers hopped out, and then a team of Sectoid aliens popped out of a portal to join them. The mixed unit deployed toward the dilapidated outbuildings of the freeway rest area.

"This is astounding," said Marin, staring in shock.

Gilmore looked at him. "Why are aliens at Vail Pass?"

Lopez pursed her lips. "Hmmm," she said. "Maybe they saw all the purple dots."

Marin nodded. "Maybe they're tracking psionics too," he said. "That makes sense."

The researchers watched as the troops fanned out and climbed a slope toward the remains of the rest area's main shelter. Suddenly, the Sectoids halted. Clearly, they sensed something. Their trooper escorts crouched, tense now, weapons raised.

The first video ended.

* * *

Marin exchanged puzzled looks with his team. He said, "How many Sectoids did you count?"

"I saw three," said Lopez.

"Three," agreed Gilmore.

"Me too," said Marin. "Three. That doesn't account for all the psionic wells we saw in the overhead map."

Lopez reached to click on the second video. All three of them gasped at the opening seconds.

"This is five minutes later?" asked Marin.

Lopez nodded. "Good god," she said.

The outbuildings were in flames. ADVENT Troopers and their Sectoid overlords were taking fearsome incoming fire, seemingly from all directions. Most of the squad already lay twisted on the ground twitching or dead. The surviving troopers appeared to be in a state of panic, either cowering or making futile attempts to flee. Meanwhile, the Sectoids had conjured a spherical telekinetic field around them that was deflecting fire.

"They're dead meat," said Lopez.

Gilmore nodded. "It's beautiful, man."

Marin squinted in disbelief at the video. "They're terrified," he said.

"Wow," said Lopez, twirling her cap backward and leaning closer. "Yeah, you're right." She reached out and tapped the Stop button. "Look at those guys by the wall. Totally freaked out."

"Incredible," said Marin. "Those are highly trained, psi-directed ADVENT soldiers. Yet look how *rattled* they are. Even the Sectoids are reacting erratically." He reached past Lopez to the console and dragged the video's scroll box back and forth, replaying the opening segments. "Look at that! It has all the signs of a powerful psi panic attack."

"Who could do that?" asked Lopez.

"I'm sure I don't know," replied Marin.

"Are the aliens attacking their own units?" asked Gilmore. "I mean, nobody else has that kind of psionic punch."

"Let's watch again in overlay," said Lopez.

She dragged the scroll box back to the opening frame. This time she activated the psionic detection filter and let the clip play again.

Gilmore pointed. "Purple glow to that incoming fire."

"Psionic enhanced, all of it," said Marin. "Very advanced. Certainly beyond the weaponry we've been able to produce."

They watched the last few seconds of the grim video. The remaining ADVENT Troopers were cut down as a swirling purple storm of psionic energy engulfed the Sectoids, shattering their defensive sphere. Then a final volley of weapons fire tore them to slimy pieces.

Stunned, Marin said, "That vortex was a Rift attack."

Lopez looked up at him. "Only Elders can conjure those," she said.

Marin nodded. "This is just . . . unbelievable." He squinted, remembering. "We had just one GEIST volunteer, our most advanced candidate, who could throw a Rift. Twenty years ago."

Gilmore suddenly pointed at the screen. "There!" he cried. "Look!"

Several cloaked figures, murky and indistinct, drifted through the trees on the opposite ridge. They looked like ghosts.

And then the second video ended.

"Gilmore," said Marin. "Download the next segment."

Gilmore looked sheepish. "Uh, there is no next segment," he said.

"Why?"

Gilmore and Lopez exchanged a glance.

"Well, Will," said Gilmore. "Per instructions, the sensor minicam shuts down when it stops getting discrete psionic pulse readings."

Marin pinched the spot between his eyes. "And what idiot gave you such idiotic instructions?" he asked.

"That came right from the top," answered Gilmore.

Marin took a deep breath.

"Don't *ever* listen to me again," he said. "Am I clear on that?"

"Clear as vodka, boss."

Marin stared up at the video window. They had just witnessed something extraordinarily significant. This could be a game changer. Somebody out there had harnessed psionic power and turned it with lethal fury on the alien overlords of the planet. Were they human? Rebel aliens?

Who were these guys?

Lopez reached out and squeezed Marin's arm. She said, "Just so you know, you're the best idiot I've ever worked for." She smiled. "One of the best, anyway. Probably in the top ten or twenty, definitely."

"Thanks."

Amused, Gilmore slid the chair he'd been standing on up to the control console. Then he sat in it and looked up expectantly at Marin.

"Same," he said.

Marin licked his lips. It was something he did unconsciously whenever he had a tremendous amount of work looming ahead of him.

He said, "Start analyzing this data."

Gilmore saluted. Lopez was already tapping away.

Marin walked straight across the lab to Dr. Tygan.

"Richard," he said. "I have something you need to see right away."

Tygan brightened. "Is it good news?"

"Not sure," said Marin. "Central needs to see it too. Can I call him down?"

Tygan said, "He's out in the field today. Took one of the Skyrangers, so it must be important."

"In the field? Doing what?"

Tygan smiled. "I believe he's reaching out to the locals."

6
TRACKS

BACK IN NEW SAMARA, Alexis Petrov sat, eyes closed, on her bedroll. Cold winds wailed down Apache Peak through the naked aspens outside her tent. She hadn't moved in two hours. Time slowed like a slurry flow.

There were quiet voices outside.

"Volk is ready."

"Now?"

"Yes. He's in council with the visitor, but he wants her to join them."

For hours, Petrov's mind had flipped between two channels. In one, she saw the Indian Peaks etched sharply against blue sky above the settlement. This was the inner place where she'd been instructed to go. Earlier, the camp psychologist, Veng—Reapers jokingly called him "Medicine Man"—had led her through a series of directed visualizations. He called it CBT trauma management.

The other channel, of course, was the vivid, bloody hunting camp under Devil's Thumb.

Whenever her inner eye went there, her instructions were to turn around and walk until she could see white mountains and blue sky again.

"What if I want to stay and fight?" she'd asked.

"You will someday," Veng had replied. "But for now, trust me, you need to walk away."

Petrov had lost squad mates in combat before, beloved ones. This was war. Loss was inevitable. But before, it was one here or two there. Months apart, sometimes even years. Nothing like this—not for her and not for the Reapers. So many dead in one encounter. The camp was in shock.

Nobody blamed her. Here at New Samara, everyone offered comfort. But they needed a narrative, clearly. Who did this? Twenty hunters lost to a single, shadowy entity? Petrov saw CK, Jean Natter, and everybody else on that hunt. Reapers she'd known for years and considered family. They'd fought together, saved each other. Huddled countless hours around campfires. Knew each other's stories.

One by one, they stopped by Petrov's tent, the living and the dead.

They offered comfort but sought explanation.

So far, she'd turned them all away. But now it was time to face Volk.

* * *

Konstantin Volikov—known to all Reapers simply as "Volk"— was a burly, bearded, intimidating man. His predecessors were resilient Russian refugees from Samara who'd resettled to Alaska in the previous century, founding a remote village north of Talkeetna that they named East Volga. The hunting and fishing was spectacular, and the town became a base camp for expeditions to the twenty thousand-foot summit of nearby Denali, the most prominent peak in North America.

But when the first alien troops probed the Alaska Range in 2014, Volk—then just twenty-one—responded by organizing a zealous resistance effort. East Volga's remote location probably kept him alive during his reckless early days as a rebel leader. The aliens' general lack of interest in snowy, mountainous regions—areas that ADVENT now labeled the Wild Lands—had given Volk's fledgling cell the breathing room it needed to study the enemy, develop effective tactics, and flourish.

Volk's clan became known as the Reapers. Over the next decade, high-country resistance cells along the length of North America's spine united under his leadership. Eventually, he moved the Reaper base of operations to its current location: New Samara in Colorado.

A bazaar-like tent city, New Samara was easily the largest Reaper encampment, home to nearly 350 warriors and their families. Volk named it in memory of his family's city of origin in Russia. Before the alien invasion, old Samara had been a bustling waterfront capital on the banks of the Volga River, a major economic and cultural center with a population of 1.1 million citizens.

Now it was a desperate, burned-out slum cowering on a polluted waterway.

* * *

Petrov's assigned chaperone for all three days since the Devil's Thumb incident was a senior-level Reaper field commander named Kate Starling. She wasn't much older than Petrov, but she had a comforting, motherly manner. It was remarkable, given her well-known ferocity in combat.

Starling slid her hand gently around Petrov's arm as they strolled across camp to Volk's command tent.

"He's a badass but not a monster," she said.

"Volk?" said Petrov, with a slight smile. "I've made reports to him before."

Starling squinted one eye. "Not like this one," she said.

"True."

"I've fought with Volk for thirteen years," said Starling. "And by that I mean"—she pointed straight ahead—"we fought side by side." Then she pointed at Petrov. "And we fought face to face." She grinned. "I'd want nobody else at my side in battle. And I'd want *anybody* else in my face in a hot argument. Even a Chryssalid."

Petrov nodded. "I'm nervous," she admitted.

"Just tell it to him straight," said Starling. "Volk hates arrogance and modesty equally."

Petrov nodded again. "I'm good," she said.

"Good."

Volk's command post was a big twelve-by-twenty-foot wall tent with an internal carbon fiber frame and a stovepipe jacked through the roof. Volk's personal bodyguard, a veteran sniper named Bobby Chung, sat on a stool under the entrance awning. He held up a hand.

"Hey, Kate," he said. He nodded at Petrov.

They waited as Chung ducked inside. After a second, he opened the flap for them.

"Have a seat," said Chung, pointing at a bench.

Volk sat at a table staring at the screen of an open laptop. Next to him sat a weathered, dark-looking man in his fifties. He wore a commando sweater and had a deep vertical scar running down his right cheek.

"Yes, John, we've seen them," Volk was saying as they examined the blue-lit screen. "Not friendly encounters, mind you. But we haven't exchanged gunfire, if that's what you're asking."

The man, John, nodded. "This is the best close-up shot we got," he said. "Clearly, they're not human. Or not entirely human, anyway."

Volk frowned. "But you say they kill aliens?"

"Boy, do they," said the man with a dark smile.

"Well," said Volk. He pulled at his thick beard with thumb and forefinger. "Normally I'd say the enemy of my enemy is my friend." He pointed at the screen. "But these guys are too ugly to be anyone's friend."

John laughed. "I think that's racist, buddy."

"Right." Volk nodded. "So what else do we know?"

John tapped at the screen. "Our intel says they speak our language, and it seems they call themselves . . ."

"Skirmishers," interrupted Kate from the bench.

Both men looked up at the women.

"Hello, Kate," said Volk with a grin. "Did you come to correct us?"

"Only when necessary," she replied.

"John, this is my tactical field commander, Kate Starling," said Volk. "She's the smartest fighter in this camp. In *any* camp, actually."

"Hello," said John.

Starling nodded curtly. "I know who you are," she replied. Her tone wasn't entirely congenial. Curious at this, Petrov glanced over at Kate's impassive face.

Volk sat back in his chair. "Sorry, John, my people still have bad feelings based on misconceptions," he said. "They don't know you like I do."

The man nodded. "It was a time of betrayal," he said. He spoke now with careful precision. "I understand the feelings. A lot of us took a shiv in the back from people we trusted. It's hard to get past that."

Petrov sensed an intensity behind this exchange that she did not understand. After a brief uncomfortable silence, Starling took a deep breath. "Look," she said. "If Volk vouches for you . . . that's good enough."

When the visitor smiled, his scar twitched. "Can I ask what you know about these Skirmishers?" he asked.

"I've never seen one," said Starling. "Other than sending down occasional sentries, they keep to the high passes. We've heard some crazy stories in Leadville and other high-country settlements. Almost like Bigfoot sightings. Mostly just tavern talk, I figure."

Volk leaned back forward. "Kate, get your people to make a full report on anything they've seen or heard on Skirmishers."

"Alright," said Starling.

Volk looked at Petrov. "Ah, yes," he said. "John, let me introduce you to one of my team leaders, the one I told you about. Alexis Petrov, this is John Bradford, central officer in charge of operations at XCOM."

"*XCOM?*" blurted Petrov.

Now Starling's attitude made sense. Many Reaper lieutenants saw XCOM as part of the global cabal that cut a deal with the alien Elders and sold out the human race. They suspected that the newly resurrected XCOM was at best weak and at worst a haven for collaborators and spies.

But then Petrov noticed Bradford's expression had changed.

"You're the one?" he asked, eyes narrowed.

Petrov looked confused. "What?"

"The one who saw him," pressed Bradford.

"Saw who?"

Bradford frowned. "The Hunter." Confused, he looked over at Volk.

Volk stood up. "She doesn't know about the Hunter. None of my soldiers do." There was a catch of emotion in his voice. He stepped around the table and approached Petrov. Next to her, Kate Starling stood up too. She put a light hand on Petrov's shoulder.

Volk leaned in close to her face.

"Tell us your story," he said. "Then we'll explain what you saw."

* * *

When Petrov finished, Volk told her of two other Reaper hunting parties ambushed the previous week.

Both were farther north, deployed from camps in the Roosevelt National Forest north of Estes Park. In each patrol—three Reapers in one, four in the other—the ambush left a lone survivor. Their reports were disturbing. At Volk's request, Bradford had provided an XCOM forensics team to help in the postmortem.

After analysis of survivor testimony, ballistic testing, autopsy, and other results, the team concluded that a single marksman firing an extremely high-powered sniper rifle was responsible for all five kills. Moreover, the shooter exhibited a seemingly impossible mobility, flanking targets with stealth and stunning speed.

Neither survivor saw the shooter.

"I'm interested in something you described," said Volk. "After you cleared your vision, you saw a dark figure in the trees, correct?"

"Yes," said Petrov.

"But his head was above the trees? Like a giant?"

"Not exactly," said Petrov. "They were pygmies."

"Pygmy trees?"

Petrov nodded. "It was a stand of pygmy pines," she said. "Right on the creek. That's why we pitched camp on the opposite bank." She looked over at Bradford. "Pygmy trees tell you that bedrock is just under the surface. Hard to pitch your tents securely."

"Noted," said Bradford with a thin smile.

Volk was pacing. "After we . . . recovered your hunting party, we did an initial scan of the site," he said. "It was difficult, as you can imagine." He stopped to stare at the tent wall. "But we'll go back and check out those trees."

"I can tell you right now they're exactly six feet tall," said Petrov.

"How do you know?"

Petrov cleared her throat. "CK Munger, my best trigger man, walked into the stand when we pitched camp," she said. "He's six feet tall. The trees were his exact height. He made a joke about it is why I remember." After a pause, she repeated, "He *was* six feet tall."

Volk said, "We're looking for some way to ID this shooter, other than, you know . . . a big guy with a deep voice."

"His head and entire chest were above the trees," said Petrov. "I would estimate nine, ten feet tall."

"Good god," said Starling. She turned to Bradford. "Why did you call him the Hunter?"

Bradford reached out and closed the laptop. Then he stood up and slung it under his arm.

He said, "That's what he calls himself."

"You've talked to him?" asked Starling.

Bradford laughed. "No," he said. "He's left a few calling cards, so to speak." He raised his dark eyebrows. "It's clear that he wants his presence well-known in your community. To sow fear."

Starling nodded. "Hence the designated survivor of each massacre."

"Precisely."

Outside, the sound of aircraft engine whine slowly revved up. Volk reached out and shook Bradford's hand. "Thanks, John. I know you have to get back."

"Yeah, I've got a recon team gearing up," said Bradford. "We have reports of ADVENT heavy transports hauling construction modules over the Divide."

"That's not good," said Volk.

Bradford pulled a flight headset from a utility pocket and hooked it over his ear. "No, it's not good—for any of us. We think they're building some sort of high-altitude facility over on the Western Slope."

Volk's eyes widened. "Maybe a network relay?"

"Maybe."

"If so, let's kill it."

All Reapers despised the insidious flow of disinformation and fear aired daily from ADVENT's hidden Network Tower. Volk had long ago designated the tower's destruction as a primary strategic desire. In a daze, Petrov listened to them share thoughts on ADVENT's global propaganda efforts to slander the Resistance.

"Any luck tracking down those rumors of your Commander?" asked Volk as he walked with Bradford to the tent entrance.

"None," said Bradford.

"You know we'll help if we can," said Volk, raising his rumbling voice over the engine whine. "I hope it's true. He was a great man."

Bradford just nodded and ducked out of the tent.

Seconds later, Petrov heard the XCOM aircraft rise above the camp, then bank away.

* * *

Petrov sat now, stunned.

Kate Starling had rejoined her on the bench. Volk stood behind his table. He put his hands flat on it. Then he leaned forward, head down.

He said, "I'm sorry, Petrov."

Petrov stared at him. "I'm the designated fear carrier," she said.

"It appears so," he replied.

Her eyes darkened to anger. "The Hunter," she said, teeth clenched. She turned to Starling.

Starling shook her head. "This is something new," she said.

"Entirely new," agreed Volk.

Petrov turned to him. "Let me find him," she said.

Volk shook his head no. "This is not on you," he said.

Petrov jumped up, hands on hips. "How can you say that?"

Volk's eyes flared. He rose up to his formidable full height.

"This is not on you," he repeated, slower. "You are restricted to camp. You'll take a four-week leave of recovery. Understood?"

She dropped her hands. After a few seconds, she took a breath and said, "Yes, sir."

"I've called in all of our hunting parties," said Volk. "We have plenty of provisions for winter. Everyone stays in camp for now." His look was fierce. "Now go. I have much to do."

Starling took Petrov's arm and guided her outside. Chung, the guard, nodded as she passed. The women walked across camp without speaking. Cooking smells filled the air, the smell of game, and it sickened Petrov. When they reached her tent, Starling held open the flap.

She said, "I'll see you for tea in the morning."

"You don't have to do that."

"Oh, I'm afraid I do," said Starling.

* * *

Petrov sat on her bedroll.

Shadows floated across the tent's sun-facing walls as Reapers walked past outside. Each shadow was a nine-foot specter. No amount of visualization could change that. Replaying the slaughter in loops, Petrov stayed and fought every time, trying every shooting angle so that CK's head wouldn't explode and Jeannie Natter wouldn't be slit open like a sausage casing.

Every tall shadow would haunt her—awake or asleep, it didn't matter—until she took action.

Shortly after nightfall, Petrov cleaned her rifle, sharpened her knife, filled her canteen, and stuffed her travel pack with dried food. She strapped a small tube tent and bedroll to the pack frame.

Avoiding campfires, Petrov slipped out of New Samara.

* * *

She hiked cliffside trails along the Indian Peaks—Apache, Navajo, Kiowa—in darkness for five slow, painstaking hours before pitching the tent in Arapaho Pass.

At dawn, Petrov woke and continued east. She moved fast, knowing Kate Starling would visit her tent soon, find her gone, and inform Volk. They would guess where she was going, so she wanted a solid head start.

By sunrise, following the old Fourth of July Road, Petrov was past Nederland. By nine, she could see Bear Peak ahead, backlit by the sun.

By noon, she was atop Devil's Thumb, where her hunt would begin.

* * *

Tracking is part method, part instinct.

Even the best-trained bloodhound is stymied when the physical trail goes cold. A good tracker sometimes needs to look up from the ground to find other signs of the prey's destination or purpose.

Petrov was a good tracker. In fact, it was her specialty, one reason she led Reaper hunting parties.

Traces of the Hunter were plentiful on Devil's Thumb, and the physical trail was easy enough to follow at first. But the first meta-clue came before Petrov even descended the spire. As she stood at the lip, she heard a distant droning from the northeast.

She watched as two big-shouldered ADVENT cargo transports slowly approached, then passed directly overhead, loudly. A thick, armored section of prefabricated military-grade wall dangled by cables beneath each craft. Robotic gun-turrets bristled at the corners of each wall section.

She watched them fly to the southwest.

As they did, she remembered Central Officer Bradford's words: *We think they're building some sort of high-altitude facility over on the Western Slope.* Judging from the cargo, ADVENT was making a military move into the high country. A forward operating base.

Maybe the Hunter was spearheading that move. Maybe he was recon. Search and destroy.

Maybe that's his base.

Petrov eye-marked the exact spot where the big haulers disappeared over the snowcapped peaks of the Divide. Then she pulled out her mapbook and plotted their course. She knew that ADVENT flew as the crow flies, locking dead-on to final destination coordinates. After all, they controlled the skies completely; no need for evasive waypoint flying. So she drew a straight line from Devil's Thumb southwest into the Elk Mountains.

If she lost the Hunter's trail, she would follow the line as closely as possible, given the terrain.

Then she descended the Thumb and examined the ground. The first footprints were just off the rocky talus. The Hunter's tracks were large and deep, and his footwear left a distinctive sole mark. In places they disappeared completely, sometimes for fifty meters or more. Then they'd reappear with a long, two-grooved landing skid.

The tracks led southwest. She followed them for an hour. They disappeared completely in a meadow where a patch of ground was blackened by engine burn. A transport pickup.

She stood on the spot for a minute, then consulted her map.

The Elk range was wild, rugged country, accessible only via backroad passes and trails. She estimated at least two days, maybe three, just to get across the Divide.

As far as Petrov knew, no Reaper had ever been back there before. She would be the first.

7

CONTACT

FOUR DAYS AFTER the grisly discovery at Tuhare Lake, leaders of all twelve Skirmisher tribes in the Intermountain West region answered a summons from Mox. Each brought a squad of their best soldiers, as requested.

The meeting convened at the new Wildcat camp location. After the ADVENT attack at Turquoise Lake, the Wildcat crew had hauled the entire village west, deeper into Colorado's Western Slope. They'd resettled in gladed terrain next to a creek-fed basin near the bottom of the old Snowmass Village ski runs.

The first evening, Darox and his Kestrel tribesmen made their grim report to the gathering. Their presentation included disturbing images of the massacre scene. Then Mox spoke.

"I bring greetings from Betos," he announced. "I also bring news and a proposition."

Sitting behind Mox, Darox ran his fingertips lightly over the scar on the back of his head. He glanced at Mahnk next to him, who looked miserable. Mahnk had finally completed his neurochip extraction rite just the day before. The procedure made him so nauseous that the post-rite ceremony had to be postponed.

"We face two existential threats," said Mox. "We propose a mission that may address both. As the humans say, kill two birds with a single stone."

A few of the tribal leaders exchanged puzzled glances. Most Skirmishers took things very literally. Metaphors and human tropes were often lost on them.

"We have all heard of the Assassin now," continued Mox. "You have seen her image. Speaking with you individually today, I have learned that her Kestrel ambush may be just the latest in a series of recent incidents."

"Let her come again!" cried a female voice in the back. "We will tear her apart like tissue paper!"

This got the audience fired up; there was a metaphor they understood. Mox patiently waited out the yelling and chest thumping, then raised his hand.

"Revenge will be ours, brothers and sisters," he said calmly. "Hear me out."

Darox watched closely. Mox had a natural, unforced command presence. The crowd immediately quieted, and respectful faces turned to him.

"Our long-scouts recently discovered an ADVENT hive of activity not eight miles from here," said Mox. "Maybe you have heard reports or seen the heavy transports passing to the south." He made an angry fist. "Those are not reconnaissance patrols. This is a material incursion with, I fear, permanent designs."

Murmurs rippled across the audience. "So it is a combat outpost?" called out a voice.

Mox raised his hands.

"We do not have details yet," he said. "But it appears to include a troop garrison. Sentries have spotted ADVENT soldiers patrolling passes under the Maroon Bells. It may be an attempt to establish a provincial center."

Another voice called out, "About time they imposed some order on these unruly mountain settlements."

This prompted general laughter.

Then a chief with fearsome face tattoos stood up in the front row. "Could this explain the appearance of the cowardly Assassin?" he bellowed.

"It could be related," nodded Mox.

"The alien monster clearly hates Skirmishers," said the tattooed chief. "Perhaps ADVENT is building a mountain base for her, with the express purpose of wiping us out."

"There is much we do not know yet, Praag," said Mox. "But you could be right."

Darox glanced over at Koros and Rika. The hike back down from Tuhare Lake had been excruciating. Both carried their grief and shock in stoic silence, but it was clearly rooted deep, particularly in Rika. Over the past days, he'd spent much of his time with them. Camp rituals kept them busy, but they needed more. They needed vengeance.

Mox took a few more questions, then got to the point.

"We will drive ADVENT from our mountains," he said. "But we must flush out this Assassin. The new outpost may be the monster's lair, her base of operations. But we believe that, even if it is not, an assault there may lure the Assassin to support the facility. And if she does, we will be ready, trap laid."

Darox suddenly stood.

He said, "A point, sir."

Mox turned to him. "Yes?"

Darox indicated the other Kestrels sitting beside him. "We respectfully ask to be included in any expedition to the ADVENT outpost."

Mox looked at Koros, then Rika. After a few seconds, he nodded. "Granted. Anything else?"

"No, brother," said Darox.

* * *

The strike force was large by Skirmisher standards. Most tribal activity was hit-and-run, conducted in small squads. But Mox put together a full platoon-sized detachment of five separate clan-based squads, each with six warriors—five soldiers plus their tribal chief as leader. The rest of the visiting tribes would help the Wildcat cohort secure the new settlement location, setting up sentries and checkpoints in the passes surrounding Snowmass.

Mox also added a four-man recon fireteam to the strike force. Led by Darox, the team included Rika, Koros, and Mahnk. Rika looked sullen when Mox announced the assignment, but she made no comment.

Mahnk, of course, was thrilled. "We spearhead an assault on a heavily fortified position!" he exclaimed. "What could be more glorious?"

"Our role is recon, brother," said Koros, amused. "I suspect our job will be to find the secret back door."

Mahnk chortled. "And then bash our way inside!"

Koros secured two ten-round shotgun mag-loaders into the ammo pouch on his combat vest. "We will be right behind you, friend."

Darox laughed. But Rika stood up, grabbed her gear, and walked toward the supply tent. They watched her go.

"She is taking it hard," said Koros.

"Understandable," said Darox.

Mahnk's smile disappeared. "I will apologize," he said, rising to follow Rika.

Koros grabbed Mahnk's arm.

"No," he said. "She needs to be solitary with her thoughts. That is how she is. How she's always been." He looked at Darox. "I do not envy your job, Captain."

Darox thought a moment. Then he asked, "Did she lose anybody special?"

Koros shrugged. "We are all brothers and sisters," he said.

"Yes, we are all kin," nodded Mahnk, blinking.

"But sometimes there is someone special," said Darox.

"Really?"

"Yes, Mahnk." Darox looked over at the other troops gearing up for battle. "We are mostly human, after all."

* * *

Scout intel placed the ADVENT "hive" near the old quarry town of Marble. Although the straight-line distance from Wildcat was eight miles, Marble sat on the far side of a nearly impassable line of high peaks. The next morning, Mox's adjutant Loka was monitoring the regional weather forecast coming out of New Denver.

"Heavy snow squalls at higher elevations," she reported. "Not good."

"How soon?" asked Mox.

"Soon," she replied. "You do not want to be on a rock face above ten thousand feet."

So Mox led the Skirmisher detachment on a fifty-six-mile detour, following old roads north through El Jebel, then curving around the high peaks back south. They skirted the notoriously lawless settlement of Carbondale. From there it was straight up the Crystal River Valley to Marble.

Skirmishers were hardy and fit, trained to jog double-time for long stretches. Even so, it was nearly sundown when they finally spotted the old town up ahead. They hadn't seen a single ADVENT patrol or flyer on the entire trek.

Mox called together his squad leaders.

"We camp for the night," he said. He pointed out a wooded spot near the river. "No fires."

As the full detachment plunged into the pine trees, Mahnk moved up beside Darox. Snow flurries swirled through the branches.

"This is a little odd, don't you think?" he asked quietly.

"How so?" replied Darox. He found a protected hillock, so he dropped his pack and slid off his sleep sack.

"Too quiet."

Darox nodded. "It is quiet."

"No ADVENT anywhere."

Darox opened his canteen and said, "Our scouts tracked the transports here."

"Well, I just used my scope to check ahead," said Mahnk, pointing down the road. "Marble looks completely deserted. Not even stray dogs."

"Our scouts do not make mistakes, brother."

"But then where is the outpost?" asked Mahnk.

Suddenly, Mox's voice boomed through the trees: "Recon!"

Darox widened his eyes. "I think somebody wants us to find out."

* * *

Fifteen minutes later, weapons drawn, Darox's recon team dashed along Crystal River to the town perimeter. Marble was indeed abandoned. All structures and roads were in utter disrepair. It looked as if nothing had been disturbed in decades.

"Nothing but ghosts," said Mahnk, gazing at a toppled building with a sign that read, "Crystal River Jeep Tours."

"Another dead town," said Rika abruptly. "How shocking."

The others looked at her. It was the first time she'd spoken in hours. After a few seconds, Koros said, "These mountains are unforgiving."

"Unforgiving?"

"Yes, sister."

She said, "Everything is dying up here."

Koros looked around and said, "All I see is life everywhere, living on."

Rika gave him a dark look. "Are you serious?"

Koros nodded. "I am."

"Well, aren't you the happy fellow."

"I am, sister," said Koros. "Although I admit I do wish that life cared more about me." He shouldered his shotgun. "When I die, which could be any minute now, I will probably curse life for going on as if I never existed."

Mahnk, who'd been following the conversation with a confused look on his face, said, "Wait. What is that sound?"

They all listened.

Suddenly, a wave of loud mechanical clanking and grinding rolled across town. It came down a cracked asphalt road marked "3C" on a road sign.

"Heavy machines?" said Koros.

They took off at a trot along the roadside. After a half mile, the asphalt veered rightward, following a small creek up a side canyon. Another series of sharp, grinding sounds reverberated off the canyon walls. Darox stopped and checked the GPS map in his wrist intel unit.

"This is Yule Creek," he said. "The road runs a mile farther to an old marble quarry."

"Ah," said Koros, "that explains the town's name."

"It explains a lot actually," said Darox, scrolling up a report.

Yule marble was very famous marble, it turned out. The

immense, flawless deposits of metamorphosed limestone, found only in this canyon, were considered the purest in the world. Yule marble had been used to build the exterior of the Lincoln Memorial in Washington, DC, and the Tomb of the Unknown Soldier at Arlington National Cemetery, two iconic human monuments that didn't mean much to Darox, though he understood they had great symbolic significance.

More important to the moment: The report he read noted that thousands of massive eight-by-eight-foot marble blocks had been carved out of the interior of Whitehouse Mountain just up the road. This left a vast, luminous cavern, geometric and perfect, lined with 99.5 percent pure calcite.

"The entire mountain is a marble-lined vault," said Darox, still reading.

"What?"

Darox looked at Rika. "Perhaps ADVENT is using the quarry to build some kind of super-secure storage facility."

"To store what?" she asked.

"Good question."

Suddenly, about a mile up the canyon, the lights of an ADVENT Troop Transport rose vertically into sight above the tree line. A second one followed, then a third, then two more. They spread into a loose V formation and, with noses dipped, accelerated slowly down the canyon toward them.

The team scrambled into the trees and watched the boats ferry past.

"Five transports," said Darox.

"That's a lot of troops," said Koros.

Mahnk smiled. "Enough for robust combat."

The sky was darkening fast. It was another mile to the quarry site, and the deep growl of heavy machinery grew louder every step of the way. Twice they had to avoid haulers rolling down the road. To circumvent an ADVENT sentry checkpoint, Darox led his team across Yule Creek and up a rock ramp on the opposite canyon wall.

The ramp curved onto a narrow ledge with a spectacular overview of the bustling construction site.

Mahnk was ecstatic. He whacked Darox's arm.

"Look at that!" he said. "So many targets."

"This is astounding," said Koros, eyes bright.

Towering floodlights illuminated an area the size of two football fields. A fleet of huge vehicles—cranes, transport trucks, diggers and earthmovers, a colossal plasma drill—rumbled near a large, glowing cave entry cut into the mountainside. Guarding the opening was a stout security bunker topped with ADVENT robotic turrets.

"Look for the Assassin," said Darox.

Dozens of ADVENT troops and other personnel stood in clusters everywhere. A handful of Chryssalids crouched in positions around the area's perimeter. But after a few minutes of scanning the site, nothing resembling a nine-foot-tall female blade-master was spotted.

"We do appear to be vastly outnumbered," said Koros, counting armed units.

"Not even the element of surprise could make this a fair fight," said Rika dryly. "Not that I care."

Darox took a knee next to her and leaned on his Kal-7.

"Why don't you care?" he asked.

Rika shrugged. "The more jabbers and bugs down there, the more I can kill."

Darox said, "So you want to wade in and kill as many as you can."

Rika didn't answer.

Darox glanced at Koros, who stepped up next to Rika as well.

"That sounds suicidal, sister," said Koros.

"I am not *planning* to die," said Rika. "I just don't care if I do."

Darox said, "We are a recon fireteam. You know what that means."

Rika looked at him with cold silver eyes. "I do not need a condescending lecture on recon tactics."

"Then tell me," said Darox. "What is our core operating principle?"

Mahnk couldn't stand it. He burst out, "We kill for each other, not for ourselves!"

Darox looked at him. "Well, that *is* one way to put it," he said.

"Because we are kin," said Mahnk with emotion.

Koros put his hand on Rika's back.

"I call you sister because I will do anything to make sure you survive," he said. "In return, I trust that your tactical decisions won't compromise my health."

"Exactly!" cried Mahnk. "A kamikaze attack will only get us *all* killed."

Darox knew Rika understood. They were all highly trained soldiers. They'd all learned that the standard fireteam's tactical doctrine—"Overwatch, Suppression, Movement"—was based on a well-known psychology. In the crucible of combat, especially at close quarters, a soldier's survivability and will is more heavily influenced by the fear of letting down one's comrades than by "courage" or abstract concepts like patriotism or liberty.

Rika stood up and faced them. "Here is an operating principle for you," she said. "Everybody go crank yourselves and leave me alone."

Mahnk grunted. "Good plan," he agreed.

"I like it too," said Koros.

Darox turned to evaluate the bustling, well-lit vista below them. "Fair enough," he said. "Let's get back to camp. We need to help Mox rethink this undertaking."

He was about to lead the way down the rock ramp when a small rockslide of pebbles rattled onto the ledge from above. Everybody froze. Then they trained their guns upward as a deep voice called down.

"Don't shoot, folks," it drawled, calm but firm. "We have ten rifles, a scatter laser, and a big-ass machine gun locked on your heads right now."

Darox aimed at the voice. "We are not ADVENT," he called upward.

"Well, son, I figured that," replied the voice. "So just set down those weapons. Then we can have us a chat over good Kentucky whiskey."

Darox nodded at the others. Reluctantly, they laid their weapons on the ground and raised their hands.

"Oh, put your hands down," called the voice. "You're not prisoners. Yet."

At this, a slight smile spread across Koros's face.

"You are not Reapers, are you?" he called up.

"Hell, no," said the voice. "Do I *sound* like a damned cannibal?"

* * *

Skirmishers often ran into pockets of so-called "Resistance" types scattered across the high country. Most were just roving bands of subsistence hunters, ragtag survivalist cults, or a few ranch families banded together to defend a crumbling compound.

In most confrontations like these, an armored Skirmisher patrol would absorb a sudden volley of incoming fire and then quickly lay waste to the poor fools who engaged. But Darox could sense that this was different. Very different.

"Follow that footpath to your left," called the voice. "It runs up here."

As Darox led his team up the path, he called out, "Can you identify yourselves?"

"We can," replied the man.

The Skirmishers traversed a granite outcropping and then climbed up onto a small plateau. There, a dozen heavily armored soldiers crouched behind boulders, eyes to their gunsights. Darox nodded.

"My name is Darox," he said, "and I cannot drink whiskey."

A dark figure chuckled and stepped forward.

"I'm sorry to hear that," he said. "I'm Captain Roy Thibideaux, XCOM special forces. This here is my Alpha squad." He took a few steps closer and pulled off his helmet. He looked to be in his fifties. "Say, you fellows don't look exactly *human* to me," he said.

"We are human," said Darox. "But that is not all we are."

"What are you then?"

"Hybrids," said Darox. "All of us were once ADVENT soldiers. I was an officer."

Now Thibideaux stepped up to him. "Am I meeting my first Skirmisher by any chance?"

"It is very possible."

"Dang."

The XCOM captain studied him for a moment. Then he waved his arm to the side.

"Guns down," he said.

Behind him, the soldiers lowered their rifles. Thibideaux turned to face them.

"I mean all the way down."

His squad exchanged puzzled looks for a second. Then, one by one, they placed their weapons on the ground.

"Come on out here, kids. I want you to meet some of the most badass alien killers in the Wild Lands."

Darox couldn't help but smile at this. When he did, Thibideaux looked at him and said, "Well now, that's a Louisiana grin right there, brother." He grinned too. "That's human enough for me."

He glanced over at Koros. "Say pal, you mentioned Reapers. What do you know about them?"

Koros shrugged. "Not much," he said. "Just stories."

Thibideaux pushed out his lower lip. "I hear they like to kill aliens too, which is good." His face twisted. "But then they eat the bastards, which is downright sickening." He turned back to Darox. "So, Darox is it? What exactly are you boys doing up here?"

At this, Rika stepped forward.

"Is it not obvious?" she said. "And by the way, we are not *boys*."

The captain raised his eyebrows. "My apologies, ma'am," he said. He gestured to his soldiers, who were shuffling up awkwardly. "I got four badass gals myself on this squad. Eloise here is my suppression specialist."

A six-foot-tall blonde who'd been lugging a minigun nodded at Rika. She said, "Cap makes me carry the big gun."

"Anyways, my question still stands," said Thibideaux.

Darox said, "We tracked ADVENT cargo flights here." He glanced over at the sprawling, floodlit construction site. "This scope is most disturbing."

Thibideaux nodded. "Agreed," he said. "My story is the same. You look like a recon unit. How many more of your people are up here?"

Darox hesitated. During his years with ADVENT, it was assumed that XCOM was dead, buried. But rumors of the legendary agency's resurrection had bounced around mountain communities for years, according to veteran Skirmishers he'd met. Alpha squad certainly looked legitimate. Their equipment was top-notch and well-maintained.

But still, he couldn't just offer up intel to a stranger.

Thibideaux noted his hesitation.

"I gotcha, son," he said. "Listen, I've got two more squads back on the ridge, Bravo and Charlie. We're thirty soldiers total. Some of our best people. I've got Grenadiers with cannons and plenty of demolitions. We might be able to handle a base assault." He pointed down at the cavern opening. "But this is bigger than we expected. Who knows what the hell they got inside there? I fear some elite alien bastards may be supervising this fancy dig."

Darox paused. Then he said, "Captain, we have a sizeable force as well. Let me take you to my commander."

Thibideaux turned to his team. "Maintain surveillance. Corporal Blunt, you come with me," he said to the woman he'd called Eloise. "I want you watching my back."

"Yes, sir," she replied. "Can I bring my big gun?"

"I would say that's up to our host," he said.

Darox started traversing the outcropping to the rock ramp that led down to the canyon floor. He said, "We dodged several ADVENT patrols coming up this canyon. I admit I was wishing for a big gun."

Blunt hefted her gleaming minigun.

"Your wish just came true, silver eyes," she said.

* * *

An hour later, they sat in a Skirmisher command tent. Mox's eyes glittered darkly.

"Are you suggesting some sort of quid pro quo, Captain?" he asked.

Darox tried to read Roy Thibideaux's face in the bluish glow of the clover-shaped LED lantern that hung above the table where all three sat on camp stools. This tent was much larger than the field sleepers. But like all Skirmisher tents, it had a Mylar lining to block infrared signatures and dim the glow of interior lights.

"XCOM has intel you folks want, clearly," replied Captain Thibideaux. "And it sounds like you know a few secrets too, commander."

They'd been comparing notes on ADVENT and the alien hierarchy for more than an hour. Darox's evaluation of the XCOM captain was still evolving. The man was refreshingly honest and good-humored, yet Darox sensed a caginess too. No doubt Mox did as well. XCOM had an agenda. But then, everybody fighting for survival in a conquered world had an agenda.

"Before we make a deal, tell me more about this Assassin," said Thibideaux.

"We have seen only the aftermath of her foul work," replied Mox. "She leaves no survivors. We have no eyewitnesses."

"Sounds like a damned blood demon."

"She has immense powers, clearly," said Mox. "Only the rare Elders we have faced have been so lethal. Her stealth ability is terrifying. And she conveys a threat specifically to Skirmishers. She seems to see us as particularly odious traitors, no doubt because of our alien genetics and ADVENT training."

Captain Thibideaux considered this information.

"Let me report this to my central officer," he said. "Maybe we can help track the fine lady." He smiled. "Well, commander, I think we've got some common objectives."

"We both want this facility destroyed," said Mox.

"Absolutely," said Thibideaux.

"And yes, as a former ADVENT Elite captain, I do retain certain classified secrets I could share," said Mox.

Thibideaux grinned. "Well, there's just one secret we *really* want," he said.

"I understand," said Mox. "I might be able to steer you in the right direction." He turned to Darox. "What do you think, brother?"

This caught Darox by surprise. But he sat up and said, "If we work together to cauterize the Yule Creek canyon, I expect it could establish the basis of a permanent partnership. We could share not just intelligence secrets, but also resources and tactical support."

Captain Thibideaux gazed at Darox.

"Cauterize the canyon," he repeated. "Damn, I like that."

"I share DNA with the aliens," said Darox. "But I have come to see their incursion as a systemic infection of this planet."

Mox smiled darkly.

"Well said, brother," he murmured. He looked at the XCOM captain. "Shall we make a plan?"

Thibideaux put his elbows on the table and clasped his hands thoughtfully.

"Yes, but before we start," he said, leaning forward. "Are you boys sure you won't try a slug of Blanton's Single Barrel with me?" He patted his hip pouch. "I find that it helps lubricate the prefrontal cortex."

Mox hesitated, then said, "Well, Captain, the offer is appreciated. But . . . in our ADVENT training seminars, it was often emphasized that alcohol is incompatible with alien blood chemistry."

"Incompatible?" growled Thibideaux. "With Blanton's Single Barrel? How could that be?"

Darox shrugged. "Apparently, hybrid blood oxidizes alcohol directly into formic acid."

"What happens?"

"You go blind, then you die."

Thibideaux frowned. "I don't see how that's any different from humans."

8

QUARRY

AT SUNRISE the next morning, XCOM Grenadiers opened fire on the ADVENT troops and machinery clustered in the excavation site's staging area. The carnage was swift and staggering. Perched on the ledge where Darox had first met Captain Thibideaux, XCOM squads Bravo and Charlie unleashed a fusillade from the canyon wall opposite the quarry entrance.

Meanwhile, the five Skirmisher squads swarmed the site's perimeter defenses, blasting hissing Chryssalids into ribbons of seared flesh and butchering ADVENT Troopers crouched in unfinished perimeter bunkers. At the same time, XCOM Alpha squad quickly overwhelmed security checkpoints down the canyon and secured the entry road to the site.

As the battle raged below, Darox and his recon team worked laterally across the mountainside nearly one thousand feet above the quarry opening. Koros, in the lead, hopped over a narrow but deep crevasse. As the nimblest climber, he took point on most technical routes.

"I thought I was joking yesterday about finding a secret back door," he said.

XCOM camera drones had marked activity in a darkened couloir cut into the back slope of Whitehouse Mountain. Intel analysis had suggested it was an alternate exit from the quarry cavern; the ravine was cleared of debris and graded, creating a smooth exit ramp.

Mahnk was deeply annoyed. "Do you hear that gunfire?" he grunted. "That is where we should be. Not up here, stumbling around like goats."

"Goats do not stumble, idiot," said Rika, giving him a push up a boulder pile.

Darox brought up the rear. Despite Mahnk's complaints about the climb, it had been relatively easy going; Whitehouse was a moderate slope with natural switchback access routes. But the climb was the least of Darox's worries.

He'd been assigned two objectives. The first task—to interdict the enemy's emergency escape route—made sense for a small recon team. But his second directive was more complicated and fraught with risk.

Koros led the way up a tree-lined saddle to a promontory with a clear overview of the couloir.

"Exfiltration point below," he said, pointing.

"Any movement?" asked Darox.

"Hard to see."

The cleft was still in deep shadow; the sun hadn't yet risen over the towering Maroon Bells to the east. Darox pulled out his ADVENT binoculars, wide-set for hybrid eyes, and handed them to Koros, who trained them down the ravine. Then Darox unclipped a small device from his utility belt. It was a fist-sized metal module with a handle and two short, needlelike prongs on top.

Rika stared at it. "Good god," she said. "Is that it?"

Darox nodded.

"I've never seen one before," she said.

Mahnk, hands on knees, refused to look. "Please do not let me see it," he said. "I will disgorge my breakfast right down the mountain."

Koros reached out. "Can I see?" he asked.

Darox handed the device to him. Koros held it reverently and examined it.

"Amazing," he said. "The instrument of our liberation." He turned to Mahnk. "Don't you want to see why you're a freethinker today?"

"No," said Mahnk, staring in the opposite direction. "I do not."

Koros handed the device back to Darox. "You have used it before?" he asked.

Darox looked slightly sheepish. "Yes, but not live," he said.

Koros widened his eyes, amused. "What did you practice on? Melons?"

"Cadavers."

Only a select few Skirmisher recruits were trained to wield the PRF electrode needles. The best stun-baton fighters—often former ADVENT officers like Darox, but not always—learned how to deploy the needles in the base of an unconscious ADVENT Trooper's skull and trigger the ablation sequence that disabled the subject's neurochip.

Unfortunately, the procedure didn't always work. That added to the suspense of each "liberation event."

Suddenly, they heard a series of large explosions from the battle in the Yule valley far below.

"That may be the main security bunker," said Darox, clipping the PRF back onto his belt, then taking back his binoculars from Koros. "If so, we may get our first runners soon. Let's set up."

"This is a good overwatch position," said Rika, gazing down into the fissure.

"Agreed," said Darox. "You stay here."

Koros pointed at the high, walled-off end of the darkened couloir. "See that gray square at the bottom of the headwall?" he said. "That is likely a garage exit."

Darox nodded and slid an old ADVENT-issue stun baton from its loop on his belt.

"I will set up near that," he said. "I want you and Mahnk in cover down here on this end." He pointed to a jumble of boulders near the ravine's open end not far below Rika's position. "If a regiment bursts out of that door, for god's sake stay down and let them pass. But if it's a squad or smaller, suppress them, and I will try to liberate a few of our misguided brothers from behind."

"Ha! This is more like it!" said Mahnk with relish.

"What if the Assassin emerges?" asked Koros.

Rika's eyes flashed darkly at him. "Then it is time for a glory kill," she said.

Darox shook his head. "No. If that happens, all other orders are suspended. We stay hidden, we contact command, and then we track her. Understood?"

Rika moved to her position at the tree line.

"Understood," she said.

"Activate headsets, red frequency," said Darox. "No chatter."

Koros and Mahnk skidded down the gravel slope and hustled into cover among the boulders. After a few seconds, Darox sprinted into the ravine up the narrow, graded exit passage. Twenty meters in, he began to question the sanity of his plan; he was completely exposed from all three cliff walls of the rift. The only cover near the big gray door was in a puddle of icy water behind a lone boulder.

As Darox splashed into the spot, he noticed a flash of movement up high on the headwall to his right. He tapped his earpiece.

"Anybody see that?" he whispered.

"See what, boss?" replied Koros.

"Something moved," said Darox. "Above the door. Right on the cliff."

"I see nothing," replied Koros.

"Nor do I," said Mahnk.

"No visuals marked," reported Rika.

Darox stared hard at the spot. He was sure he'd seen movement. He pulled out his binoculars and trained them on the spot. Nothing. He lowered them. Then he saw something slowly edge out from behind a rock column on the precipice. He raised the binoculars again.

A hooded, human figure was aiming a scoped sniper rifle. At him.

Darox looked down. A red laser targeting dot shivered on his chest. After a brief instant of panic, he had a calm, clear realization: If this shooter wanted him dead, he'd be dead already.

Slowly, Darox raised the binoculars to his eyes again. Then his silver eyes grew big.

Two more hooded human figures, pistols drawn, were sneaking up behind the sniper.

Darox stood up.

Instinctively, he began waving one hand at the shooter who was targeting his heart. But before he could see what happened, the big metal door in the headwall clanked loudly, then rattled open sideways on rollers. Darox dived back behind the boulder just in time.

Seven Chryssalids clattered out of the mountain, clearly in a big hurry.

9

ANOMALY

THE AVENGER BRIDGE was always a high-alert zone. But when Dr. Marin reported as ordered to the flight deck, the intensity had rotated off the dial.

The flight crew was feverishly running through a preflight checklist. The gunnery officer and his team stood at the ship's gun station, prepping the Avenger's fire-control system. In the middle of the bridge, gathered around the holographic Geoscape globe, Central Officer Bradford and his tactical command-and-control team (called C2) stared up at the four ceiling-mounted monitors with maniacal focus.

"Will!"

Marin turned to see Dr. Tygan waving him over to the communications console against the starboard hull. He hurried to join the chief scientist, who stood behind a row of technicians sitting at the comm stations.

"Man, it's buzzing in here," said Marin. "What's up?"

"This is remarkable," replied Tygan. "Roy Thibideaux's team found the ADVENT forward operating base. And it's *huge*."

Marin's eyes grew big. "That's good news, right?" he asked. "Or maybe not?"

"It's good we found it," said Tygan. "The aliens are building some kind of massive storage tank inside a mountain."

"For what purpose?"

"Well now, that's the mystery," replied Tygan.

Marin glanced at the Geoscape. "Where are we going?" he asked. "And why am I here?"

Tygan smiled. "We're going to Colorado," he said. "And we need your psionic sensors."

Marin nodded. "Sure," he said. "Why?"

Bradford moved to join them. "Dr. Marin," he said with a nod of greeting.

"I'll let Central explain," said Tygan. He stepped over to the radar post.

Bradford was even more no-nonsense than usual. "Before we commit to a base assault, we need to know what our troops are up against," he said, his phrases clipped tight. "If the enemy has a bunch of new-breed Sectoids or, god forbid, an Elder or two in there, we need to know about it."

"That makes sense."

"Yes," said Bradford. "Can your sensors penetrate, say, a marble-lined cavern inside a mountain?"

"Oh yeah," said Marin, nodding. "No problem."

Bradford looked skeptical. "Really?"

"Our instrumentation could probably measure psionic wells in the mesospheric mantle a thousand miles down." Marin closed both hands, then flicked them open. "I mean, psionic energy pops like firecrackers. It's very potent stuff. In the same ballpark as gamma-ray bursts, the most intense energy sources in the universe."

"Okay," said Bradford. "So, what do you need for a psionic scan of our target site?"

"I need about two minutes of piggyback time on the ADVENT psionic network," said Marin. "Thirty seconds to find the right satellite and another ninety for the scan."

"And what do you need from us to acquire this network access?"

"Nothing."

"Nothing?" Bradford's voice was getting slightly louder with each exchange. "Really? You need nothing."

"Oh, we've had network access for months," said Marin. "Just punch a button. But we can't stay very long. It would risk detection."

Bradford gave him a dark look. "This all sounds far too good to be true, Dr. Marin."

Marin shrugged. "I got this kid, Gilmore, downstairs," he said. "Guy's a genius with this sort of thing."

"Whatever," said Bradford. "How long to get this scan done?"

"Give me the ADVENT site coordinates, and I'll zap them down to the kids," said Marin. "We'll have the scan on your scopes in, oh, about seven minutes." Marin glanced at his watch. "Well, maybe eight if the Avenger is on the move. Are we taking off soon? Sure looks like it."

Bradford just stared at Marin for a few seconds. Then he said, "Yes, we are taking off soon."

Marin frowned. "Well, that might delay the scan lock by a minute or so," he said.

"That's disappointing," said Bradford.

Marin couldn't quite ascertain Bradford's tone. But he said, "I'll get my crew right on it."

Bradford pointed to a woman at the radar console.

"Check with Maggie for the coordinates," he said. "And Doctor, I'm more concerned with accuracy than speed, so . . . take an extra forty, fifty seconds if you need it."

"Thank you, sir," replied Marin. "I doubt it will be necessary."

Bradford's mouth twitched upward at both corners.

"This is the most enjoyable conversation I've had in months," he said. "Maybe years." He turned away and rejoined the C2 team at the main monitors.

Marin shrugged. "Okay," he said.

* * *

Ten minutes later the site scan was displayed on one of the console monitors. The ADVENT forward base was clean of psionic signatures.

"Interesting," said Dr. Tygan. "No psionic units at all?"

Marin stared at the monitor. "That's what it looks like."

Next to him, Bradford stood with folded arms. "Maybe they know psionics are detectable," he said. "And they don't want to be detected."

Marin stroked his chin. "Wow," he said.

Tygan and Bradford turned to him. "What is it, Will?" asked Tygan.

Marin's eyes narrowed as he thought.

"Listen," he said. "Think about that video from Vail Pass I showed you the other day, the mysterious massacre of the ADVENT platoon. Downstairs, we watched that entire sequence over and over."

"It was remarkable," said Tygan.

"Yes, well, the Sectoids in that detachment were clearly on super high alert from the moment they debarked from their transport," said Marin. "They were looking for something. Then, boom, they get slaughtered by assailants wielding astounding psionic powers with very distinctive spectroscopic readouts."

Tygan nodded. "Maybe the aliens got psionic readings via some form of spectroscopy too and were hunting down the source?"

"Exactly," said Marin.

"So how does that apply to this forward base?" asked Bradford.

"Maybe this mysterious new cabal of psionic masters can track psionic activity too," said Marin. He turned to Bradford. "Just like you suggested, the aliens may be trying to avoid detection. To keep this base secret from their new tormentors." He looked at Tygan. "My people and I think what happened on Vail Pass was a slightly more dramatic version of what our sensor data has been telling us for weeks. This has been happening all along the Continental Divide. We just didn't have the context to grasp it."

"What do you mean?" asked Bradford.

Marin walked up to the Geoscape and pointed to the Rocky Mountain region.

"We crunched all of our readings from the past two months," he said. "Hot spots popping up all along the range from Canada on down."

Bradford and Tygan stepped up next to him. They all gazed at the shimmering hologlobe.

"Psionics appear in a scan," said Marin. "Soon after, other psionics sort of *arrive*. There's a jockeying for position, it seems . . . rapid, chaotic . . . and one by one, dots get snuffed out. We thought maybe it was just the unstable nature of psionic energy . . . or just a bunch of satellite noise. We had no idea what sort of actual events our scans were depicting."

Tygan nodded. "Alien psionic units, maybe attached to ADVENT patrols, are the first dots," he said. "And they're getting detected, hunted down, then wiped out by these unknown entities."

At this, Bradford turned to face Marin.

"We need to find these people," he said. "And get them on our side."

Marin thought for a second. Then he asked, "What if they're not human?"

"Who cares?" said Bradford. "They kill aliens. I've got thirty-five ghoulish hybrids out on the battle line right now."

He jabbed his finger toward the overhead monitors. "They call themselves Skirmishers. They have snake noses and silver eyes the size of saucers. And guess what? *They are now our allies.*" Bradford pinched his forehead and closed his eyes as if in pain. "For today, anyway."

"Well, they clearly hate the aliens as much as we do," said Tygan.

"Right," said Bradford. "There's a Resistance movement out there. It's extensive but scattered in many pieces. Our job is to pull it all together, preferably under XCOM direction." He looked at Marin. "You've got a new job, Dr. Marin."

"Find the psionic people."

"Yes."

Marin nodded. "Okay."

Suddenly, a C2 officer called out from the tactical console on the port hull.

"Quiet on the command deck!" he shouted. All chatter immediately ceased. "Central, sir, Captain Thibideaux is ready for kickoff. All three squads locked and loaded, Grenadiers ready to launch. Skirmisher units are on the base perimeter, and we've got recon up on the ridge at the escape hatch. Waiting on your green, sir."

"Green light," said Bradford without hesitation.

Speaking into a slim microphone on the console, the C2 officer said, "Sick 'em, Roy."

"Battle stations, everyone," called Bradford.

Marin, unsettled, glanced over at Tygan. "Should I go back to the lab now?"

"Hell, no, Will," said Tygan, staring up at the current live feed, an overhead shot of the ADVENT base from a hovering drone camera. "This is the biggest XCOM move in twenty years. You want to tell your grandkids you were on the Avenger bridge the day we started winning the war."

Marin smiled big. "I like your optimism."

"Other than my scruffy lab, it's all I've got right now," said Tygan.

Bradford called out, "Captain Maddow?"

From the front of the bridge cockpit, the Avenger's pilot flipped a switch and said, "Yes, sir, ignition switch set. All systems go. Ready for liftoff on your call."

"Let's go to Colorado," said Bradford.

On-screen, the live image shuddered as concussion waves from the first volley of XCOM cannon fire hit the camera.

* * *

Dr. Marin found the actual warfighting aspect of XCOM's mission both fascinating and horrifying.

As an evolutionary biologist, he understood the exigencies of survival, the dark buried roots of violence, war, even genocide. And the pitiless mass slaughter of Earth's innocent civilians had long ago snuffed out any concern over the ethics of XCOM's cruel medical experimentation on alien prisoners.

Intellectually, he also grasped the necessity of XCOM's brutal tactics on the battlefield. But the violent and bloody immediacy of the drone-fed imagery was still unsettling. Bradford's C2 team had multiple live video feeds running on the XCOM bridge monitors, shifting quickly between helmet-cams of various troops in the fight. The chatter was impressively calm and professional as C2 took field input and directed combat operations in real time. But every few minutes, one video feed would go black just as another feed recorded an ADVENT counterstrike across the field. A momentary hush would fall over the situation room: another good soldier down.

"Confirmed," called the C2 casualty officer after one report. He turned to Bradford. "Four down, sir."

"Ten percent is acceptable," replied Bradford. "Press ahead full."

"Roger that. I've got a specialist patched in."

"Let's hear him," said Bradford.

A panting voice reported, "Two are stabilized and good for medevac. But we lost two."

"Roger, we will authorize Skyranger pickup once the enemy turrets are KIA," said the C2 officer. "Until then, keep those folks breathing, sergeant."

"Will do," replied the voice. "Out."

The good news was that the ambush seemed to have caught the ADVENT base defense entirely by surprise. Enemy units that survived the initial bombardment were soon overwhelmed by the Skirmisher waves sweeping up both flanks. At one point, Captain Thibideaux's voice blared over the speakers. C2 put his feed on the main monitor.

"By god, these hybrids are good," he exclaimed. His helmet-cam view bounced as the captain forded Yule Creek, advancing into the target environment. "Damned if they didn't roll up both sides faster than grass through a goose. We're already hitting the bunker."

The last obstacle to the quarry cavern was the fortified ADVENT security bunker guarding the entrance. Heavily armored robotic turrets were installed at each corner of the roof. The rotating guns spewed red-hot Gauss rounds and could take a lot of punishment. Nailing them would require a masterful demolitions effort.

"Roger that, Roy," said Bradford with a tight smile. "Are you good?"

"Yeah, I'm good."

"How good?"

"It's a Cajun clambake, Johnny."

Roy Thibideaux was the only person aboard the Avenger—and probably in the entire world—who could call Bradford "Johnny" and get away with it.

On-screen, Thibideaux's head turned just enough for a helmet-cam glimpse of Corporal Eloise Blunt to his right laying down ferocious suppressive fire with her minigun. Gazing at the monitor, Marin watched in awe; the woman was tall and mighty, swinging the blazing gun muzzle side to side. Her armor had distinctive black stripes slashed across its camo pattern. She was also a hellish bartender in the Avenger lounge when she took her rotation.

Suddenly Marin's beeper went off. He flipped open his shipboard communicator.

"Hey, Bonnie, what's up?" he asked.

Lopez hesitated, then said, "Uh, we just ran a follow-up scan on the base area."

Marin immediately ducked over to an unoccupied alcove near the exit door. "I don't like your voice right now."

"Something's coming," she said.

"Crap," said Marin. "The assault is fully engaged."

"It looks big."

Marin glanced over at Bradford. "Since the Avenger is on the move, we can probably risk another good scan," he said. "Let's make sure we have something solid before I drop a bomb on this situation room."

"Dialing it up now, boss," she said. "Where should I send the files?"

Marin found an unused console station and punched up its network address. "Sending you an address now," he said. "Buzz me when the scan's done, send it here, and we'll talk. Is Gilmore there?"

"Boss, he sleeps in our equipment alcove."

"What?"

"He's always here is my point."

"Okay, tell him I'm not taking an abort recommendation to Central just because we saw some scary purple dots." Marin glanced up at the monitor feed just in time to see two XCOM

Rangers pinned down by turret fire. Powerful Gauss rounds were shattering the rock slab where they hid. Rock chips flew like confetti.

He said, "Tell him I need more than purple dots."

* * *

Fifteen minutes later, Marin watched nervously as his favorite bartender, Lieutenant Danny Roman, launched an EMP grenade with uncanny accuracy onto the only ADVENT turret still operational on the bunker rooftop. The bluish detonation disabled the gun's firing mechanism long enough for Bravo squad's concentrated cannon fire to shred its armor.

After a few seconds, the turret exploded in an orange fireball.

"Well done, kids," called Captain Thibideaux over his radio feed. "Johnny, we are at the gate."

"Acknowledged," replied Bradford. "Are you taking fire through the entrance?"

"Hang on," said the captain.

There was a pause. Several different feeds were linked to monitors in the bridge. All of them had grown silent.

"Listen to that, XCOM." It was Thibideaux again. "We are inside, and it's a church in here."

On-screen, the monitor transmitting the video feed from Thibideaux's helmet-cam went blinding white. After a few seconds, the light ratio adjusted. The feed showed a massive cavern with towering, snow-white walls. Construction scaffolding lined the lower levels. Two 80-foot cranes and assorted other vehicles were parked nearby.

Other than the machinery, the vast space was deserted.

"Gosh," reported Thibideaux. "Either we killed them all out front, or the rest skedaddled. I suspect the latter."

As if in response, the sound of heavy gunfire could be heard in the background. It sounded distant.

"Captain, we're hearing a firefight way up high on the ridge," reported the Alpha squad leader, a Ranger lieutenant named Dobbs.

The C2 team started tapping console buttons.

"That must be the Skirmisher recon team at the back exit," said the tactical officer.

Bradford watched the monitor. "The vault is empty because the rats are abandoning ship," he said. "Can we get a drone up there for a picture?"

Suddenly, Dr. Marin's station monitor beeped with an arriving file. On-screen, he popped open a map scan sent up from Lopez. When Marin saw it, he quickly flipped open his cell-comm and called her.

"Bonnie, is this right?" he asked quietly.

"It is what you see," she replied.

"They're right on the mountain!" said Marin.

"Indeed they are, boss."

Marin caught Dr. Tygan's eye and urgently waved him over.

"What is it, Will?" asked Tygan as he approached.

Marin pointed at the scan.

"We've got something very, very psionic arriving from the east," he said.

10

COULOIR

WHEN THE CHRYSSALIDS burst from the mountain, the strange humanoid whom Alexis Petrov had been studying through her scope was, oddly enough, waving to her. She watched as he lunged into cover just before seven ravenous insectoid killers clattered past his boulder. His dive was graceful for such a large man, if "man" he was. It reminded her of CK Munger.

They'll smell him, she thought.

At that moment, she felt the cold barrel of a pistol on the base of her skull.

"Please don't move, Alexis," said a female voice quietly.

"Lay down your rifle," said a male voice. "Please."

Petrov took a breath, then smiled. "You're so polite, how can I refuse?" she said. She put the rifle down. "Can I face you?"

"Slowly," said the female. "Hands up, please."

Petrov raised her hands and rotated to see Mia Vo, a woman she'd hunted with numerous times. Next to Mia, also holding a pistol trained on Petrov, was Joe Epstein, one of the most jovial and gregarious Reapers in New Samara. Seeing him point a gun at her, she fought back laughter but couldn't control her grin.

"What's so funny, Petrov?" he asked. "You know I've been wanting to kill you for years."

At this, all three of them cracked up. Mia Vo's laugh was one of the best things in camp, especially when she tried to suppress it, as she did now. The two lowered their weapons. Epstein was about to speak again when several bone-chilling Chryssalid shrieks drew their attention.

Petrov turned to see the bugs fanning out in a circle around the humanoid below, who scrambled atop his boulder. The door in the mountain rolled shut with a loud metallic clang.

"Damn, they found him fast," she said.

Vo and Epstein stepped up beside her, frowning.

"This will be ugly," said Vo.

"It's not a very fair fight," agreed Epstein.

Then it hit Petrov. "You guys were sneaking up behind me," she said.

"Indeed we were," said Epstein, nodding. "Which reminds me—technically, you're under arrest, comrade."

"That guy down there was trying to warn me," said Petrov. She turned to Epstein and Vo. "He saw you coming."

They hesitated only a second, then all three Reapers quickly slipped their Vektor rifles from their slings. They set up, called targets, sighted, and took out three Chryssalids with clean one-shot kills in the first volley.

* * *

Atop the boulder, Darox had wielded his Kal-7 Bullpup. Via headset he was ordering his team to remain in hiding—an order they would disobey, of course—when he saw green eruptions of alien blood spurt upward from the mandible-chomping heads of the three Chryssalids trying to sidle around his left flank. All three bugs dropped dead immediately. It was easily the finest shooting exhibition he'd ever seen.

"Koros?" he radioed. "Mahnk? Did you do that? Who did that?"

Darox looked down the graded path toward the boulder pile at the ravine exit. Both Skirmisher brothers, howling loudly with shotguns drawn, burst out of the rocks and sprinted directly at the remaining Chryssalids. Rika was sliding down the slope behind them, looking as angry and regal as ever.

"Okay, I like these odds much better," said Darox.

He swiveled and fired his shotgun at the nearest bug. The blast tore off one of its hind legs, but it kept coming, lightning fast. When the beast reached the boulder, it tried to leap up. But the missing leg hindered its jump and it landed short, slashing with its poisonous talons at the rock just below Darox.

This left the monster helpless against Darox's point-blank follow-up shot.

The other three bugs had turned to face the Skirmishers charging loudly up the couloir. Although Chryssalids stood a full two meters high, they moved with frightening speed, rarely seeking cover as they dashed straight at targets. They tended to work in packs, sending in one to draw attention while others darted to flanking positions.

As a result, during the initial alien invasion in 2014, most soldiers (including XCOM operatives) had been trained to engage Chryssalids from a distance whenever possible. But Skirmishers were different. They had claws too.

One bug hissed and jabbed its slavering mandibles at Mahnk, who deftly stepped aside. Gleaming silver Ripjack blades abruptly extended from his wrist gauntlet. With great relish, he plunged them into the creature.

Mahnk's strike tore a gaping hole in the arthropod's sleek black exoskeleton, and greenish gore poured out. Then Mahnk thrust upward, enlarging the gruesome gash, and the Chryssalid convulsed in shrieking agony. In just seconds it fell dead, leaving only two bugs alive: one small and purple with glowing eyes, the other larger and deep black with a more humanoid torso and head.

"Two breeds of the same vile insect!" shouted Mahnk, his claws dripping with bug blood. "I want them both as trophies!"

Darox realized his position atop the boulder gave him no real advantage—Chryssalids could leap twenty vertical feet with ease. He dropped to the ground and maneuvered behind the screeching purple bug, which now stood in a face-off with Rika farther down the path. The larger, black Chryssalid tried to dance sideways around Rika for a flank attack, but Koros dinged it with an impressive hipshot.

Rika fired her own Bullpup, then immediately rolled toward the rock wall to avoid the purple Chryssalid's slashing talons. Mahnk lunged to land a glancing claw-strike of his own. When the embattled bug turned to him, it seemed to realize that its options were limited. That moment of hesitation gave Darox a chance to unclip an incendiary grenade and carefully roll it under the bug's tail end.

"Live fire!" he shouted.

Everybody dived away.

As the fireball engulfed the shuddering arthropod, the black Chryssalid suddenly pounced and pinned Koros to the ground. A quick poisonous talon strike punctured Koros' chest plate before anyone could move. Then the bug's head rose up, readying its dripping jaws for a thrust into the exposed flesh, a move that would kill Koros and implant eggs, turning him into a zombified host.

But then the Chryssalid's head exploded.

Darox heard the crackle of multiple rifle reports a split second later.

He turned toward the couloir's headwall.

* * *

Up on the rock ledge, Petrov turned her head from her rifle scope.

"That was my bullet," she said.

Epstein patted his rifle. "Sorry, no, Daisy here took that one," he said.

"Wrong," said Vo. "My kill."

Petrov smiled and put her eye back to her scope. As she swung her sight across the ravine, she centered on the big humanoid again. He was gazing up at their position. After a second, the fellow raised his hand.

"He's waving again," she said.

Epstein waved back. "This is me waving goodbye," he said. He looked at Petrov. "Alexis, we need to scoot home. You heard the hornet's nest down the mountain. There's a lot of nasty fighting going on in the valley."

Petrov had heard the furious gunfire and ground-rocking explosions as she'd arrived on the rock ledge overlooking the couloir.

"They're taking the fight to the aliens," said Petrov, watching the humanoids tend to their wounded squad mate. "That's a good thing, right? Let's go say hello."

Mia Vo checked her auto-loader. "I do like the way they kill Chryssalids," she said with a wicked grin. "Up close and personal."

Petrov looked at Vo. "Mia, how long were you guys on my tail?"

"Every step," said Vo.

"Come on."

"She's not kidding," said Epstein, reslinging his Vektor. "Volk put you under full surveillance the moment you got back to your tent."

Petrov looked confused. "So why didn't you just stop me when I was sneaking out of camp?" she asked. "Why let me get this far?"

Vo frowned. "We wanted to see what you'd find," she said, as if it was obvious.

Epstein nodded. "You're the best tracker in New Samara." He stood up. "You find all the good stuff."

"Well, I didn't find the Hunter," replied Petrov. "I lost his trail days ago. I followed the ADVENT cargo flights to this place instead. The aliens are building something big and important down there. Look what they've got defending it." She stared down at the Chryssalid carcasses scattered across the ravine. Then she pointed at the humanoids. "Joe, before I left, Volk and the XCOM officer were talking about Skirmishers. You've heard of them?"

Epstein's eyes widened. "The scary high-country boogiemen we keep hearing about in the settlements?"

"Yeah," said Petrov. "Those guys down there sure look like candidates, don't they? Let's go make first contact. Like Mia said, they kill aliens real good. They might be valuable allies."

Epstein frowned. "Our orders were to track you down and bring you back safe."

Suddenly, the heavy security door groaned under them on the headwall. It started rolling open again.

"Uh oh," said Vo.

Petrov watched as the humanoids below dragged their injured mate into the boulder field at the ravine's open end. She knelt back down and raised her rifle.

"Let's get sighted," she said.

"Roger that," said Vo.

Epstein sighed. "Okay," he said.

Below them, more Chryssalids rushed out, doing their odd four-legged skitter. Petrov counted two, four . . . and then four more.

"Okay, I got eight total," she said. "Damn."

And then four more clattered out.

"Crap," said Vo. "Twelve!"

And then seven more, one by one. The phalanx of spiky, four-legged horrors was so long it stretched nearly the full length of the couloir. They stepped over their seven dead cousins without even pausing to investigate.

"Now I count nineteen," said Petrov. "This is bad. Real bad."

"We gotta lay low," said Epstein tensely. "I mean, if we open fire now . . ."

"We'll be dead," whispered Vo, nodding. "The jumpy bastards will find a way to swarm us in no time. They're relentless."

The vanguard of the Chryssalid column was clattering through the boulder piles now. Petrov could see no sign of the Skirmishers. But she knew they were stuck in the rock jumble. There hadn't been enough time for them to climb the slope and retreat through the tree line. Especially not with a wounded soldier.

The lead Chryssalid suddenly halted and rose up taller, scanning the rocks.

Some said bugs could detect the electromagnetic fields of living entities. Others said they had the alien equivalent of a dog's sense of smell—biosensors that could "sniff out" particulate residue in the parts-per-billion range. Whatever the case, experience had shown that Chryssalids had a knack for finding hidden people.

"What's the go, boss?" asked Vo.

Petrov nestled her eye into her rifle scope. "Unless you guys want to arrest me again, I'll start at the front end and work my way back," she said.

Vo smiled and aimed. "I'm keeping count this time," she said.

Epstein sighed again. Then he unslung his rifle.

* * *

Darox listened as the clattering of bony insectoid legs suddenly came to a halt.

They smell us, he thought.

He didn't know exactly how many Chryssalids gathered next to the rocks, but he'd seen enough to know his team was vastly outnumbered. He felt good about fighting in the boulder pile, where Skirmisher tactics and weapons gave them some advantage. But Koros was gasping from the poison and barely able to see, much less fight. And even if the snipers up on the headwall ledge, whoever they were, offered fire support, the odds were still not good.

He glanced over at Mahnk and Rika. They knew it too. Yet both looked entirely unafraid.

Mahnk leaned close. "Time for glory, brother," he whispered.

Darox smiled back. "Yes, it is time," he said.

He nodded at Rika, who nodded back. Koros lay next to her, and she put a gentle hand on his wounded, heaving chest. Then she slid to the far edge of the large granite slab they used for cover. Darox unclipped a fragmentation grenade and held it up. The others did the same. As the rattle of Chryssalid legs stabbing at rocky footholds grew louder, they tossed the frags over the slab.

The detonations triggered something entirely unexpected.

When Darox rose with his shotgun, he saw mayhem and sheer panic unlike anything he'd ever seen. The great Chryssalid pack was scattered and screaming, taking heinous fire from multiple sources on all three cliff walls. Meaty chunks of bug flesh flew in every direction. Darox spotted the muzzle flash of the Reapers' rifles on the headwall. But clearly, much heavier ordnance was hitting bugs, rocks, and ground with gut-wrenching thumps of concussive power.

The incoming rounds had the distinctive purple glow and carbonite odor of psionic energy.

One black Chryssalid scrambled madly over boulders and made a great leap completely over the granite slab where the Skirmishers hid. The alien bug nearly landed atop Koros; when the creature crouched and turned hungrily to the fallen warrior, it caught shotgun blasts from two directions. Then Darox rammed his Ripjack claws into its ugly shrieking mouth to finish it off.

"What weapons are these?" cried Mahnk as he grabbed a handhold and pulled himself higher up the granite slab for a better look.

"And who is up there firing them?" called Rika.

Darox tried to maneuver for a better look up at the cliffs too. "This is a psionic attack," he said.

"You mean because it is making the bugs insane?" asked Mahnk.

"Psionic energy is not just mind voodoo, brother," replied Darox. "It is a powerful physical force."

Darox recalled the fearsome punch of psionic weaponry from his ADVENT days. His squad once deployed in a raid with a rare Elder escort to a rebel laboratory complex obviously considered a high-value target. The lab's security team found out that Null Lance bolts—pure psionic energy—hit a lot harder than even a mag-slug.

"By the Elders, look at that!" cried Mahnk, slipping in an old ADVENT exclamation. "The bugs are shredded. Not one left standing."

Darox caught a glimpse of movement high on the cliffs. But then his vision seemed to fog and spin. He braced himself on the slab and shook his head.

"I am seeing purple," called Mahnk, dropping from his handhold.

Rika held her head with both hands. "What is this?"

And then, just as quickly, the haze cleared.

"That was a small dose of Mindfray," said Darox, rubbing his temple. "Somebody who hates aliens has a basic mastery of psionics." He looked over at Rika. "Amazingly, they have also channeled it into their guns."

"They just saved our lives," replied Rika.

"Yes."

She knelt by Koros and bent over him.

"Let us hope they saved his life too," she said.

Chryssalid poison was lethal given enough time to do its work. Koros needed medical care, fast. Suddenly, Darox heard Mox's voice in his earpiece.

"Recon team, report!" he ordered. "What the hell is going on up there?"

"Massive engagement," replied Darox. He provided a quick summary and added, "We have one down poisoned. Our medikits will not keep Koros breathing for long."

Captain Thibideaux's voice broke in. "Roger that, son, we got a Skyranger en route to your position for medical evacuation. Send up a smoke flare to guide her in." After a pause, he added, "That sounded like a goddamned artillery barrage up there."

Darox took a deep breath. "We have . . . unidentified heavy support units up on the ridge," he said. "Clear signs of psionic amplification."

"Psionic?" repeated Thibideaux. "Are you sure, son?"

"I am sure," said Darox. "I will make a full report when we get back down." As he stepped out of the boulder pile, he looked across the plateau. Three hooded humans were approaching. He said, "Recon, out."

The one in the lead threw back her hood. With a thin smile, she held up her hand.

Darox said, "Mahnk, send up a smoke flare for the medevac."

Reaching into his combat vest, Mahnk turned toward the trio, who stopped uncertainly twenty feet away. He pulled out a flare stick, held it up to show them, and smiled. Then he bowed deeply.

The Reapers nodded back.

Mahnk struck the flare's flint end on a chunk of granite and pointed it skyward. Fireballs shot up and exploded into mushrooms of red smoke. Meanwhile, Darox handed his medikit over to Rika. He said, "Keep his heart beating while I talk to our new rifle team."

Rika nodded, watching the hooded trio with a hint of suspicion. The lead woman stepped forward.

"My name is Petrov," she said. "Reaper clan."

"Reapers!" said Mahnk.

"This is Vo and Epstein," said Petrov, indicating them. They lowered their hoods too. "Are you Skirmishers?"

"We are," said Darox. He introduced his fireteam and added, "Our gratitude for the assistance. It was timely."

Petrov held up a small vial. "I have a salve that can leach out Chryssalid venom and help stabilize your comrade until a medical team arrives."

She handed it to Rika, who took it but said, "Our blood is different from yours."

"Not that different, I suspect," said Petrov, again with a hint of a smile. "Apply it thickly. Trust me, it won't hurt him."

As Rika applied the salve, Darox gazed up at the cliff walls. He said, "The psionic units, were they your people? Where are they?"

Petrov looked surprised. "Ours? No. We assumed they were yours."

"Interesting," said Darox. "Did you see them?"

Vo stepped forward. "We keep eyes to target until the last one falls," she said.

Petrov smiled. "True," she said. "When the ravine stopped crawling with bugs, I looked around. I saw nobody. But I had a strange, dizzy feeling at that moment."

"A psionic haze," nodded Darox. "We felt it too."

"So they covered their withdrawal," said Petrov.

"Yes."

Mahnk rubbed a small gash on his forehead. "I am sorry they are not your allies," he said.

Epstein hacked a quick laugh. "If those were our allies, we'd be in New Denver right now," he said. "Shopping."

Darox shook his head. "I have never seen such a display," he said. "I am sure the Elders are concerned."

"Screw the Elders," said Vo.

Amused, Darox said, "Agreed."

Now they could hear the rising whine of the approaching Skyranger as it zeroed in on the smoke markers. Mox's voice spoke in Darox's earpiece: "Recon team, board the XCOM jump-jet. Medical personnel will tend to Koros as you fly to our rally point."

"Acknowledged," replied Darox. "He is in stable condition thanks to some . . . field medicine." He glanced over at Petrov. "We have contact with a Reaper team."

"What?" asked Mox, alarmed. "Hostile contact?"

"No," said Darox. "They provided us with expert long-range support."

"Eleven kills," called Vo.

Mox grunted: "Reapers." After a pause, he said, "It gets more interesting up here every minute."

11

QUID PRO QUO

DR. MARIN HUNCHED over a console in the Avenger Research Lab, studying dielectric spectroscopy readouts of the psionic bursts on Whitehouse Mountain. Suddenly, the main lab door whooshed open. Central Officer Bradford and Dr. Tygan rushed in, talking earnestly.

"Will," called Dr. Tygan. "We have news. Where's your team?"

"Out in the field," said Marin. "Trying to breathe."

The Avenger had arrived in Colorado several hours after the base assault. Its initial landing site was a secluded mountain meadow deep in the back range. Bradford and Mox coordinated a round-the-clock surveillance of the shattered base site. But bizarrely, after a full week, it appeared that ADVENT was not returning . . . at all. It was as if the aliens had simply written off the base as a complete loss without a second thought. They conducted no recovery operations, no reconnaissance patrols— nothing whatsoever.

Bradford suspected a trap; he felt sure ADVENT was at least conducting satellite surveillance from their sky-net. As a result, he relied on his new Skirmisher allies, who were well trained in alpine camouflage and tactics, to keep a covert eye on the Yule Creek quarry. But finally, after days of overwatch in the Elk Mountains revealed no sign of aliens or ADVENT, Bradford flew the Avenger to an LZ closer to the base and released science teams with military escort to do a full inspection of the site.

Marin had sent Gilmore and Lopez up Whitehouse Mountain to scour the high couloir. Their job was to measure data points and collect samples and readings of the psionic activity that occurred.

Bradford pulled up a chair and sat, something Marin had almost never seen him do. Tygan grabbed a chair too, and they both faced Marin.

"This looks important," said Marin.

Bradford managed a tight smile. "It is," he said.

"How important?"

"Like, game point," said Bradford.

Tygan put his hand on the console. "We just had a quid pro quo meeting with our new friend Mox," he said. "And it turns out that, as a former high-ranking ADVENT officer, he may have information that could give XCOM an immeasurable boost in operational potency."

"It could turn the tide against these scaly bastards," said Bradford.

Marin raised his eyebrows. "Wow," he said. "But . . . why are you talking to me? Does it have to do with psionics?"

Bradford and Tygan glanced at each other.

"Well, yes," said Tygan. "But indirectly."

Bradford leaned toward Marin. "Mox has the *quid*," he said in a low tone. "You need to find the *quo*." He held out his hands. "Then we trade."

Marin smiled. "Fill me in."

Bradford was blunt. "You need to locate the ADVENT Network Tower," he said.

Marin almost gasped. "Holy crap," he said.

"How long would it take?" asked Bradford with urgency. "If the Network Tower's as powerful as everyone says, wouldn't it pop off a map scan like a freaking clown's nose?"

Marin pointed at his console monitor.

"Given the risk of detection by ADVENT," he said, "we keep our sky-net access time extremely limited. That's why it took us almost four months to scan and plant sensors in a narrow swath of North America. Yes, we could get lucky and find the Network Tower signature in one of our scans tomorrow. Or it could take a year. Or more."

"Okay," said Bradford. He folded his arms and stared darkly at a console monitor.

Marin looked at Tygan. "So . . . what do we get in return?"

"We find the Commander," said Tygan.

"What?!"

Still staring at the monitor, Bradford said, "We've long suspected that he's still alive and being used by the aliens for intelligence purposes. Plenty of clues point to that, but I won't get into those details." Now he turned to Marin. "But the data we've analyzed . . . *and my gut* . . . tell me it's true. He's out there, imprisoned somewhere, and those psionic bastards are mining his brain for operational knowledge of XCOM, among other things."

Marin was stunned. "The Commander? After twenty years?"

Tygan smiled. "Hard to fathom, isn't it?"

Marin blinked. He said, "It's like finding out Napoleon is still walking around Saint Helena."

This amused Bradford. "That's good," he said.

Marin took a moment to compose himself. Then he asked, "So the Skirmisher can find him?"

Bradford stood up slowly.

"Mox was an upper echelon guy at ADVENT command," he said. "High-security clearance. He says he once reviewed documentation of a secret alien intelligence program called XCOM Live Analytics. It made reference to things like *soft tissue archives* and *cortical processing*." Bradford stared at Marin. "Mox heard rumors about what exactly that meant."

"A living brain," said Marin.

"Yes," said Bradford. "Inside a living person, hopefully."

"So Mox knows where he is?" asked Marin.

"No," answered Bradford.

Here Tygan stood up too. He said, "However, there is a highly restricted ADVENT security facility called Omega Station that maintains all of ADVENT's classified databases. We've known about its existence for years, but our intel network never could find it."

Marin said, "But Mox can?"

"Yes," said Tygan. "He says if we infiltrate the Omega Station data core, we'll likely find exact coordinates for the black site that hosts the XCOM Live Analytics program. Along with loads of other good stuff."

"Just infiltrate the data core," repeated Marin. "I'm sure it's a piece of cake."

"Mox will help direct the strike team," said Bradford.

"Okay," said Marin. "But he wants to know where the ADVENT Network Tower is first?"

"Actually, it's a good faith offer," said Bradford. "Mox and his Skirmishers are ready to embark for Omega Station immediately . . . like, *now*. In return, he wants us to guarantee a concerted joint effort to find and destroy that tower." Bradford watched one of the console readouts, thinking for a second. Then he added, "You know, my old friend Volk and his Reapers despise the ADVENT Tower too. I really should put these guys in touch with each other."

Marin stood up. "I'll order my team back and get started immediately." He nodded at Bradford. "Tell Mox I personally guarantee we'll find that tower."

"Thank you, Doctor," said Bradford. "Your team is doing a great job."

Marin grinned. "That last psionic incident dropped right into our backyard," he said. "We should have some interesting findings shortly."

"Those guys laid waste to an entire Chryssalid regiment," said Bradford.

"It was truly impressive," said Tygan.

Bradford started to walk away but then stopped.

He said, "Look, I know this whole thing probably seems like a long shot. But getting the Commander back would be worth it." Anger suddenly lit his eyes. "I know what people think. They think, who cares, we lost. Why bring back the leader of a failed effort? But goddamn it, we didn't lose. We were winning. The Commander was orchestrating a brilliant defense of the planet against a vastly superior enemy. And then we got stabbed in the back by political leaders who sold us out." He grabbed a digital caliper and looked for a second as if he would fling it into the nearest wall. But then he set it back down. He said, "We didn't lose. We were betrayed."

"I know," said Marin.

"But nobody else does, apparently," said Bradford.

He stared at the floor for a moment. Then he pivoted and headed for the exit.

"Good luck, doc," he said.

* * *

Outside the Avenger in the Skirmisher camp, Darox stared into the crackling campfire holding a nearly full bowl of elk stew and a spoon. Alexis Petrov sat on the log next to him with her empty bowl in her lap.

Darox glanced at it. "You ate that swill?"

Petrov smiled. "I've had worse," she said.

"Really?" said Darox.

"Okay, no," she said. "This was the worst."

"It is not easy to ruin elk stew." Darox scooped up a spoonful, then dumped it.

Petrov dug into her hip pouch. "I've got some good jerky," she said. She offered him a slice, and he took it.

"Thanks."

"Man's gotta eat," she said.

Darox bit off a chunk. "Even if he is only half man."

"Right."

It had been a long hard day, and both soldiers were exhausted. After the base assault, everything was a kinetic blur, busy every waking hour—securing the site, tech salvage, camp setup, high pass patrols. Sometimes it didn't even end at night; Mahnk and Rika had drawn sentry duty and were posted south of camp. The worst of course was burial detail—many ADVENT and Chryssalid corpses to incinerate but also several comrades to lay to rest. XCOM had lost four soldiers KIA and the Skirmishers three.

Now the word going around was to gear up for another big combat operation.

"Any word yet from your crew?" asked Darox, chewing the jerky.

"Joe and Mia?" she replied. "No, but they'll be back soon." She smiled. "With a rifle platoon for the ages. Lots of good shooters in New Samara."

Now Darox smiled. "I am a big fan of Reaper accuracy," he said.

Petrov gazed over at the Avenger's silhouette, barely visible across the meadow in the day's faded light.

"I've never seen such a big aircraft," she said.

Darox glanced at it too. "Hard to believe it actually flies," he said.

They sat quietly for a minute. At ten thousand feet, the clean, dark sky glittered with two thousand sharply etched points of light. Pans clattered in the mess tent down the row. Groups of Skirmishers sat near lanterns or fires and talked quietly, cleaning their weapons. Petrov was the lone non-Skirmisher in camp. All XCOM personnel bunked aboard the Avenger, and as Petrov mentioned, her Reaper comrades had caught a Skyranger ride back to New Samara. They would report the situation to Volk and deliver an invitation from XCOM's Central Officer Bradford as well.

"I hear Central Officer Bradford wants everyone working under the auspices of XCOM," said Darox. "Reapers, Skirmishers. All the Resistance groups."

"No chance," said Petrov. "Volk takes orders from no one."

"But coordinated efforts might be more effective," said Darox.

"Sure," said Petrov. "Maybe we could all get psionic implants, and Bradford could move us around like a bunch of chess pieces."

Darox squinted at her. "Isn't that what you humans would call a low blow?"

Petrov waved her hand. "Yeah," she said. "Sorry." She set down her bowl. "What was it like, being in ADVENT? Working for them?"

The distilled hatred in the way she said "them" was unmistakable. Darox's heavy alien brow wrinkled a bit.

"Some memories are good," he said.

"But they created your memories," said Petrov.

"True," said Darox. "The historical memories, yes. But I am talking about my actual memories of ADVENT life. There were friendships. We . . . played cards in the barracks." He suddenly dumped his stew into the fire, which hissed and smoked. "I would feed this to the dogs, if we had dogs."

Petrov laughed a bit but kept pressing. "I guess I'm just wondering what it's like to be you."

Darox said, "You mean to be a half-breed?"

Petrov frowned. "Did I say that?"

"No," said Darox. "Look, Petrov, I have actually examined a great deal of the original, unaltered documentation of your human history. I do not think it is ADVENT propaganda to suggest that human culture is filled with examples of brutality, racism, and sectarian violence."

Petrov folded her arms defensively. "So?"

"So, when I was ADVENT," said Darox, "I believed I was helping stamp out the worst human tendencies in the name of peace and a better world for everyone."

"But you don't believe that anymore," said Petrov.

"Of course not," said Darox. "I would not be here if I did."

"What changed your mind?"

Darox frowned. "The moment my Skirmisher brothers disabled my neurochip, I began to see differently," he said. "For days, I sat and reexamined my interactions with extraterrestrial troops. And it became clear that every one of them was, at the core, a drone." He glared into the fire. "Unfeeling, pitiless. I saw their vicious handiwork up close. They spread terror by design. They slaughtered innocents. Firebombed population centers! All of it enforcing the psionically transmitted will of the Elders."

Petrov nodded. "So, what's the true agenda?"

Darox frowned. "What do you mean?"

"Why are they here?"

Darox looked troubled. He said, "Have you been to a New City?"

"Never."

Darox looked up at the sparkling night sky. "It is quite beautiful," he said.

"Which one?" asked Petrov.

"Any one," said Darox. "They are all the same. Clean. Efficient. Everybody's children are safe. Each city has an ADVENT gene therapy clinic that will scrub disease from your DNA." He pointed at the sky. "Are the Elders actually benevolent? Do they have humanity's best interests in mind as the Network Tower tells us every day?" He shrugged. "I do not know, Petrov. But I have seen the way their Chryssalids and Berserkers operate in the streets. That tells me something about their 'true agenda.'"

Petrov noticed a familiar figure moving toward them down the tent row.

"Captain Thibideaux," she said, rising in greeting.

"Sit back down, soldier, you've had a hell of a day," said the XCOM captain. He turned to Darox. "Honestly, son, I've never seen soldiers work as hard as you people." He looked around. "Your camp logistics are damned impressive."

Darox smiled ruefully. "We were genetically engineered to be the perfect garrison troop," he said.

Thibideaux chuckled. He turned to Petrov. "So, Gunner," he said. It had become his nickname for her. "What do *you* think of these hybrids?"

Petrov leaned forward and poked a stick into the fire, stirring up embers. She said, "Their eyes glow at night. It's creepy."

"Yes," said Thibideaux, grinning at Darox. "I imagine your ocular structure affords you enhanced night vision."

"It does."

Thibideaux gestured to the log. "Can I join you for just a moment?" he asked.

"Of course," said Petrov, sliding over.

The captain sat and turned to Petrov. "I understand you recently met my superior officer."

Petrov nodded. "Yes, back in New Samara."

"You came here looking for someone," said Thibideaux.

Petrov didn't hesitate. "I did."

The captain turned to Darox. "And a primary Skirmisher objective in hitting this ADVENT base was to lure out someone."

"Yes," said Darox.

"Unsuccessfully, it appears."

"Sadly, yes."

Thibideaux nodded. "Someone deadly, murderous, nine feet tall," he said. "Lot in common."

Darox frowned. "Are you suggesting they are the same entity?"

"That's one theory, son," said Thibideaux.

Petrov said, "One is a male sniper who kills Reapers and leaves a survivor from each massacre to bear witness. The other is a female sword-master who kills Skirmishers and leaves etchings of herself but no survivors."

"And both of the recent attacks occurred at the same time, a hundred and twenty miles apart," added Darox.

"I see you've compared notes," said Thibideaux.

"They're not the same freak, Captain," said Petrov.

"XCOM intel agrees," nodded Thibideaux as he stood back up. "But I wanted to check with you." In the flickering firelight, age and weariness seemed etched deeper around his eyes. "Your activities out here in the Wild Lands have attracted attention at the highest levels of the alien food chain. The Elders have gone and engineered goddamned super-soldiers to counter the threat you clearly pose."

Then Captain Thibideaux grinned. "Kids, I find that oddly encouraging, don't you?"

* * *

Two hours later, as Danny Roman poured soda over ice, Dr. Marin noticed a slight tremor in the bartender's hand.

Earlier, when Marin had arrived at the ship's lounge, Lieutenant Roman had been standing behind the empty bar, arms crossed, staring into space. It was the first time that Marin had ever seen Danny in any sort of repose; when the Grenadier wasn't chatting, he always kept busy behind the bar. His eyes seemed veiled and dark in a way that Marin hadn't seen before, too.

"Got any new stories for me?" asked Marin.

"Nah," said Danny. "Same old stories. They just keep happening over and over."

Marin raised his glass. "Cheers," he said.

Now Danny smiled. He relaxed his stance a bit and leaned on the bar.

"I hear things are hopping down in the lab," he said.

Marin took a long swallow of soda, then wiped his mouth and nodded. "My kids just got back from the site," he said. "Your team's work there was so clean, it gave us a ton of data to look at."

"It *was* clean," nodded Danny. "Yeah, a clean operation. Just a few glitches."

Then Marin remembered: Lieutenant Roman was Bravo squad leader. Bravo had suffered three of XCOM's four KIA casualties in the quarry assault, all due to the blistering Gauss fire of the ADVENT robotic turrets. Marin now realized that Danny had been staring at the Memorial—the far wall of the bar, covered with photos of XCOM's fallen.

"Hey, something just hit me," said Marin.

"An epiphany, doc?"

"Sure," said Marin. "A realization."

"Lay it on me."

Marin twirled his glass in the wet spot on the bar.

He said, "Clearly, the aliens admire our species. It's likely the only reason we're still alive."

"You think so?"

Marin nodded. "If they wanted Earth for something else— raw materials, minerals, whatever—they would have scrubbed humanity from the planetary ecosystem long ago. Especially given how combative we are."

"We are a pain in the ass," said Danny.

Marin rubbed his cheek. "Why else would they expend such enormous energy and resources to build the New Cities? Why are they trying so hard to make us content?" He shook his head. "It's weird. Somehow we're very important to them. They want something from us."

Danny just leaned on the bar, listening.

"Now, I think our global political sellout twenty years ago probably led the Elders to a set of faulty conclusions about our culture," continued Marin. "They think humans are craven and easy to manipulate."

"Gosh, why would they think that?" asked Danny.

Marin grinned. "We may be a craven species, but you just kicked their ass up Yule Creek canyon," he said. Then he got serious. "Hey, I was in the situation room, watching. Frankly, I wasn't sure what I was seeing, but afterwards, Central explained it to me."

"It was a bloody mess," said Danny, staring down at his hands on the bar.

"A mess?" said Marin. "Central said Bravo squad took point at the hottest vector on the battlefield. You took the heat, killed the turrets, and secured the line. That's why the rest of the strike force suffered such light casualties."

Danny shrugged. "You do what you do," he said.

"That's right," said Marin. "And so, my epiphany is this: I think it shocked the aliens. They vastly underestimated the extent of the Resistance. They had no idea we'd fight so hard to defend some remote mountainside. That's why they haven't come back."

Danny smiled and started wiping the bartop. "You sound angry, doc," he said.

"I *am* angry." He stared down at his glass. "I'm mad as hell. And by the way, what your team did, that was heroic. I'll never be that brave."

Danny said, "Come on, doc." He snapped his rag. "This war is like any other war. Sure, it's nice having brave warriors on the battlefield. But Bravo squad is winning fights because of your lab."

"What?" said Marin. "That's not . . . that's only partly true."

Danny held up his fists. "Look, if we just fight like heroes, we lose. We have to fight smart. And have better gear."

He pointed at Marin. "What you do, I could never do. I'll never be that smart."

Marin smiled. "I'm no smarter than you, pal," he said.

"True," said Danny. "But your pointy head is stuffed with a lot more . . . stuff."

"Yes, it is," said Marin, sliding off the barstool. "Okay, speaking of that, I gave myself a ten-minute break to clear my pointy head so I can be more productive." He glanced at his watch. "Time's up."

As Marin stood, Lieutenant Roman reached across the bar and grabbed his shirt.

"One more thing," said Danny. "If I ever hear an alcoholic who's been sober seventeen years tell me he's some kind of a coward . . . I'm going to punch him in the throat."

"Duly noted," said Marin.

Danny let go. "Please go save humanity some more," he said.

* * *

Five minutes later, Marin stepped off the lift and walked into the lab to find Lopez and Gilmore working furiously at the main console. Dr. Tygan stood behind them, watching intently. As Marin approached, he heard the second lift's door whoosh open behind him. He turned to see Bradford stride out with a brooding expression.

Lopez waved Marin over. "Tell me what I'm seeing, boss," she called. "This is our first look. It's insane."

Marin approached and examined a map scan video. A large purple blob pulsated in an upper quadrant.

"My god, that's the biggest signature I've ever seen," he said. "Where is this?"

Lopez paused the playback. "Roaring Basin up in Summit County," she said.

Bradford stepped up next to Marin. "I ordered a scan of the Omega Station site," he said.

"Omega Station?" asked Marin, surprised. "Mox revealed its location?"

"He did," said Bradford. "We're prepping an infiltration team for the operation. Again, I wanted a scan to see what we're up against."

Marin nodded. "So . . . infiltration," he said. "That means, like, sneaking in, right?"

"Right," said Bradford. "Mox tells us Omega Station is practically a medieval mountain citadel, heavily fortified and defended. Our preliminary intel confirms that unpleasant fact. Even a successful capture mission would likely result in unacceptably high casualties."

"Or possibly trigger a data-core self-destruct," said Dr. Tygan.

"Exactly," said Bradford. "This has to be a backdoor operation." He pointed at the paused map scan. "So . . . what am I looking at?"

Marin squinted at the screen. "What's your take, guys?" he asked his team.

"We just now compiled the scan video," said Gilmore. "Like Bonnie said, it's our first look."

"That signature is *huge*," said Lopez.

Tygan leaned in excitedly. "Do you think that's the Network Tower?" he asked. "Could we be that lucky?"

Marin stared hard at the screen.

"It is big," he said. "But come on. What are the odds? Plus, I would expect ADVENT's central conduit of psionic transmission to be more, you know . . . off-the-charts big." He gestured to the screen. "Let it play, Bonnie."

Lopez tapped a button, and the video resumed. The purple blotch continued to pulsate with an almost violent intensity. It burst outward in blooms from a central spine, like a Rorschach-style butterfly.

"Is this a single entity?" wondered Lopez.

Gilmore shrugged. "Maybe it's a bunch of psionic guys in a house," he said.

Lopez snorted a laugh. "Sorry," she said, looking up at Bradford. "Not funny."

Bradford patted her shoulder.

Tygan said, "Maybe it's the same psionic group who intervened on our behalf up on Whitehouse Mountain?"

"Not likely," said Marin. "This signature doesn't match any of the other spectral readings we've confirmed for those appearances."

After a few more seconds, the signature began to slowly migrate northward.

"My god, it's walking away," said Gilmore, rubbing his shaggy head.

"Okay, that's . . . not a tower," said Lopez.

12

INDIGO PASS

THREE SMALL TEAMS—one XCOM, one Reaper, and one Skirmisher—dropped into a secluded canyon off Indigo Pass just half a click south of Omega Station. The rift was so narrow that the Skyrangers couldn't risk landing in it. Instead, the squads used fast-rope insertion to reach the floor.

When Darox hit the ground, he called for a quick check-in from his fireteam.

"Weapons ready," said Mahnk, giving his Kal-7 a quick pump.

"I am good to go," said Rika.

Koros was still recovering in the Avenger medical bay from the Chryssalid poison. His replacement was a Red Wolf tribe veteran named Drask Calopei.

"Let's kill the bastards," he responded.

Darox gave a thin smile. "We are on stealth protocol, Drask," he said.

"Sure," said Drask. "But we can still kill a few of the bastards."

Darox nodded. "It is likely," he said. "Let's go."

Fifty meters down the canyon, three Reapers fast-roped to the ground from their Skyranger. Darox's team arrived at the point and waited.

"Darox!" called Petrov when she spotted him. She flipped up her combat goggles, and he could see she was flushed.

"Everything okay, comrade?" asked Darox.

"Hell yeah, it's okay," she said. She gazed up at the Skyranger as it disappeared over the ridge. "That was my first ride in an aircraft ever."

Darox pushed up his helmet-mask too. "It never gets old."

"You're just saying that, right?"

"I have been in a jump jet a hundred times," he said. "Every ride was a rollercoaster."

Next to Petrov, Joe Epstein unslung his rifle and started checking its scope optics. "Man, I hit hard," he said. "I didn't know fast-roping was so, you know . . . "

"Fast?" said Petrov.

"Yeah," he grinned. "Fast."

Just down the path, Mia Vo jogged toward them. "*Wooo!*" she said. "That was just ridiculously exciting."

"All our Reapers are *alert*, anyway," said Rika.

Vo grinned at her. "You Skirmishers will learn to appreciate our alertness," she said.

"Oh, we already do," said Rika.

Petrov squinted as swirling snow stung her eyes, and she pulled her goggles back down. A slow-moving winter storm had drifted through the Summit County passes, complicating the logistics. But it also restricted ADVENT surveillance, providing good cover for the Skyranger deployment. Bradford and the C2 team saw this as a net positive trade-off.

"Let's move," said Darox.

The Reapers and Skirmishers jogged up the canyon to the XCOM team's rally point. There, Captain Thibideaux and his squad of four gathered around a small, hovering Gremlin designated as Drone 526.

"Radios on," called Thibideaux over the rising wind that swirled down the canyon.

All XCOM and Skirmisher combat helmets were fitted with built-in radio headsets. But the Reapers, who rarely used telecom technology, had been fitted with external headsets. After each of the full team's twelve team members checked in on the field frequency, Thibideaux ran through a quick review of the operational plan.

* * *

With Mox's help, XCOM intel had identified a grated maintenance panel that led into Omega Station's grid of ventilation ductworks.

Four Skirmishers, led by Darox, were designated Sierra squad. They would secure exterior access to the panel located on a back wall in a narrow alley where the facility backed up to a cliff face. Then they'd secure the perimeter, which included an open meadow called the North Flats beyond the station.

Next, Captain Thibideaux and his lightly armored XCOM team, designated Xray squad, would move in behind, laser-torch the panel, and follow the duct passages into the Omega data-core chamber. There, a specialist would direct Drone 526 to hack into the ADVENT database and extract the XCOM Live Analytics coordinates.

During all this, a small Reaper rifle team led by Petrov, code-named Romeo, would perch on the canyon wall and oversee the operation, providing long-range fire support.

"You'll see everything from up there," Bradford had told Petrov during the tactical session aboard the Avenger the previous day. "I'm giving you full authority to make an abort call, Petrov. I know that's putting a lot on your shoulders, but Volk says you can handle it."

"Volk said that?"

"Yes," said Bradford. "He did."

After that tac session, Darox had come up behind her in the bridge corridor, grabbed her by the shoulders, and spun her around to face him. Mahnk stood there with him. Both Skirmishers were nearly a foot taller than her, so it felt like a shakedown by mob goons in a back alley.

"Hey, what's up, guys?" asked Petrov.

Darox said, "We trust you."

Next to him, Mahnk nodded vigorously. "Yes, we trust your vast experience," he said.

Petrov smiled uncomfortably. "Okay," she said. "Thanks."

Darox clapped her on the shoulder. "After all, you are almost three times my age," he said.

Petrov looked up warily. "Is this . . . Skirmisher humor?" she asked.

At this, Mahnk cackled like a troll. Then both hybrids turned and lumbered away.

* * *

Scrambling up handholds increasingly slick with snow, Petrov began to fear that the incoming weather might render her "vast experience" irrelevant. Visibility was already poor, and the overwatch position assigned to her shooters was still another thirty meters up the rock face.

"This is not good," said Vo, clinging to an outcropping.

"I would categorize it as bad, in fact," called Epstein, who was leading the way up.

"Just keep going," shouted Petrov. "I'll call in a report when we hit the ledge."

Five minutes later, they were in place. The shooting perch was tucked under an overhang that protected it somewhat from the burgeoning blizzard. As they unslung their Vektor rifles and set up to test the optics, Petrov tapped her earpiece to activate the field link.

"Xray One, this is Romeo," she called. "We're in position."

"Roger that," answered Thibideaux via radio. "Sierra is ready to push at the gate. Can you see them?"

Petrov put her eye to the rifle scope and scanned across the ground teams. "I see blurry people but very hard to make out who's who."

Darox's voice came over the radio. "I am waving at you," he said.

"Again?" said Petrov. "You do that a lot." She nudged her weapon sideways until she spotted a hulking figure waving from the corner of a rock wall. "Okay, got you marked."

"Ready to break," replied Darox.

All three Reapers trained their rifles on the narrow alley running behind Omega Station's central building. From their perch, they had a perfect view down its length to the opposite end. They also had a clean angle on the rooftop, where ADVENT turrets sat at each back corner. There was no safe route into the alley until those roof guns were neutralized.

"You ready, Mia?" asked Petrov.

"EMP round loaded," replied Vo. "Back-right turret in gunsight."

Petrov targeted the back-left turret. Then she tapped her earpiece again.

"On your call, big guy," she said.

* * *

Poised at the rock wall's edge, Darox and his team affixed suppressors to their shotgun muzzles. The noise reduction wasn't perfect, but in a windy snowsquall a suppressor could muffle a jarring shotgun blast enough to avoid triggering a station-wide alert.

"Ready?" called Darox to his team. All three Skirmishers gave a thumbs-up.

"Attention, all units," called Captain Thibideaux over the radio. "You know the drill. Once those guns are glowing blue, the clock is ticking. Everybody move *fast*, people. In and out, before Omega Station command sends a team to see why those turrets are offline." There was a brief pause. Then he said, "Okay, son. On your call."

Darox nodded at his team. He raised his Kal-7.

He said, "Zap those guns, Romeo."

Just like that, both corner turrets crackled as if struck by blue lightning. Darox dashed around the rocks and into the breezeway. Mahnk and Rika followed him in; Drask stepped into the alley entrance, then turned and posted at the corner.

"Backside is locked down," called Drask.

Darox sprinted down the alley toward the opposite exit.

"Nothing in the breezeway," he reported. Halfway down the passage, he glanced up and spotted the grated maintenance panel recessed in the wall. "I have the access vent marked about eight feet off the ground."

"Perfect," called Thibideaux. "Xray, get those stepladders ready."

When Darox reached the alley's end, he peered carefully around the corner at the wide-open meadow. "The North Flats are clear."

"Okay, Xray, *go, go, go!*" called Thibideaux via radio. "Alley secured. Sierra, we're drafting on you."

"Wait! Wait!" cried Rika. She pointed up at a canister with a lens, rotating twelve feet up the wall above Darox. "Is that a camera?"

Mahnk skidded to a halt next to her. "By god, yes!" he called, aiming his shotgun.

His blast shattered the canister before the lens could swivel toward them. Rika followed with a second shot that tore the canister completely off the wall. She stared at her shotgun muzzle.

"I barely heard those shots," she said. "These XCOM suppressors actually work."

"Lady, you can thank Lily Shen and her team for that," replied Thibideaux over the radio. "Best engineers on the planet."

The Skirmishers made another quick scan along the back wall and found no other surveillance devices.

"Looks clean now, Xray," said Darox.

"We're coming in fast," replied the captain.

From his corner, Darox admired the expertise and efficiency of the XCOM team. Within seconds, two specialists on folding stepladders had sliced through the access panel with laser cutting-torches. In less than a minute, the entire five-man squad and its Gremlin had disappeared inside.

"Going radio silent now," said Thibideaux quietly over the frequency.

Darox exchanged a look with Rika. She smiled, something he did not expect to see. She hadn't smiled since he met her.

She said, "These guys are very good."

Darox nodded. "They know what they are doing."

Mahnk grunted. "So far, I have killed a *camera*," he said.

"You sound disappointed."

"I am." He sighed. "But yes, these XCOM warriors are indeed impressive."

For years, the ADVENT propaganda stream flowing through their neurochips had depicted XCOM as some sort of failed terrorist cell filled with mentally disturbed malcontents. But Thibideaux's soldiers were pros. Mission prep had included a remarkably detailed XCOM intel briefing followed by a set of skillfully designed tactical field sessions.

Suddenly, Darox heard Mox's voice in his ear.

"Sierra and Romeo, this is the Avenger," he said.

"I hear you, Avenger," replied Darox.

Petrov's voice crackled over the frequency. "Copy, Avenger, this is Romeo," she said.

"Be advised," said Mox. "Heavy activity up in Roaring Basin to the north. It may be heading your way."

"What is it?"

"We do not know. Are you seeing anything?"

As Mox said this, the ground shuddered with a series of gut-churning low-frequency bursts. The air around Omega Station seemed to crackle with energy. Darox glanced up. Purplish domes of intense light pulsed upward, one after another, from behind the northern ridgeline.

*   *   *

Bradford had ordered the Avenger flown close to Omega Station for the operation. Rather than relying on scans stolen from ADVENT's network, he wanted the Avenger's own sensor bank to provide nonstop, real-time scans while the infiltration team was at work.

A few minutes earlier, the sensors had started popping with psionic activity. Purple spectral signatures bloomed all over the live map display in the bridge.

"Who the hell is that?" growled Bradford.

"Pretty sure the psionic mystery guys are back," said Gilmore, digging fingers nervously into his scraggly mane. He started typing furiously at a console workstation. "I've run the spectroscopy. Same readout. It's them."

"I count at least a dozen blips," said Marin.

"More like fifteen," said Gilmore. "Look, three groups of five."

"Maybe they've come to help again," said Lopez, adjusting the scan ratios.

"Let's hope."

And then a larger purple signature drifted down-screen from the north.

"Uh oh," said Lopez. "Our walking tower is back."

"Is it part of their crew, maybe?" asked Bradford.

The scan seemed to answer the question as the smaller blips encircled the larger spectral signature. Suddenly, all of the echoes began pulsing wildly.

"Holy mother of god," said Gilmore. "It's a battle."

Bradford leaned in closer. "How can you be sure?"

"Look," said Gilmore, pointing at his console screen. "The smaller blips are disappearing, one by one. Looks like the big guy is wiping them out."

Bradford spun to the tactical command console. "You guys hearing this?"

"Yes, sir," called an officer. "Trying to get a drone camera up there, but the snow is making it difficult."

Mox sat with the XCOM C2 team. "Contacting all go-teams now," he said, punching a button.

This triggered his exchange with Darox. After Mox issued the warning, Darox's reply was broadcast over the room's audio feed: "Yes, we are seeing heavy psionic activity over the ridge to the north." Then he grunted. "And feeling substantial concussive waves."

"We felt that one too," reported Petrov over her link. "Wow, it's knocking rocks loose up here!"

"Romeo," said Bradford. "Can you see anything from your position?"

"Not from here," replied Petrov. "If I follow this ledge around the crown, I might get a view."

"Stay in overwatch, Petrov," said Bradford. "I want your eyes on the ground teams. Send a soldier."

"Will do," said Petrov. "Mia?"

"I'm there," reported Mia over the comm.

Suddenly, Lopez started rapidly tapping her controls. "Is this right?"

On-screen, another large psionic signature drifted in from the east side. Seconds later, a third purple signature appeared from the west. Both were moving slowly toward the center of the map.

Marin looked dismayed. "That's just . . . a *lot* of psionic power converging," he said.

"*What's going on?*" exploded Bradford.

And then another voice popped onto the field frequency.

"Xray One here," called Captain Thibideaux. "Pickup was successful. Repeat, pickup successful. All units, be advised. We have the package, children, and we're coming out."

Bradford practically leapt to the tac-comm console.

"Birds One, Two, Three, this is your green light," he barked. "Light fire to the LZ with all possible speed."

"Roger that," came a pilot's voice. "All birds inbound at zero-two mikes."

Marin turned to Tygan. "What the hell are they saying, Richard?" he whispered.

Tygan's eyes were round with excitement. "Roy's team extracted the coordinates!" he said. "And our Skyrangers will pick them up in two minutes."

Petrov's voice broke in. "Mia, what do you see?"

"Snow's getting worse," answered Vo. "But holy cow, it's a battle, yeah."

Now Darox's voice broke in. "Avenger, we have big trouble in the North Flats." The sound of explosions crackled over the radio. "Taking heavy fire."

Bradford looked like he was about to explode too.

"Romeo, what's going on?" he shouted. "We need eyes! *Where are my goddamned eyes?*"

* * *

Petrov put her scope on a great, hulking shadow that stomped across the North Flats. Though murky in the swirling blizzard, the figure was clearly a two-legged mechanized walker. As it moved, it spattered laser rounds at the corner where Sierra team hid. Then it skidded to a halt.

Petrov heard Mahnk over the radio. "Is that a Sectopod?" he growled.

"It's bigger than the ones we knew in ADVENT," said Rika.

"It's charging up its cannon," called Darox. "Pull back from the corner."

Petrov could see the Skirmishers backpedal down the alley. Out in the flats with what seemed like deliberate malice, the Sectopod hunkered down, then unleashed a roaring Wrath Cannon blast. The strike tore off a large chunk of the building's corner where the Skirmishers had just stood.

Vo broke in on the channel.

"These are two different threats?" called Bradford angrily.

"That's correct, Avenger," replied Petrov.

More concussive waves rattled the rocks. Eyeing the walker down in the flats, Petrov shut off her mike and called over to Epstein.

"Joe, load EMP rounds," she shouted.

"Gotcha," he cried back, covering his mike. "It's just a big robot, right?"

"Right."

Vo couldn't hear them, so she kept talking.

"Man, heavy enhanced rounds are incoming on the big brute," she said excitedly. "Looks like the same purple stuff that tore up all those bugs back in the canyon."

As she said this, Petrov and Epstein fired EMP rounds into the Sectopod far below, which was advancing again. The walker staggered as blue energy wracked its frame. Then it dropped into a protective crouch, unmoving.

"Nice hit, Romeo," called Darox over the comlink.

"Wow, this horned monster has a shield," continued Vo. "Incoming fire-stream is splashing and flowing around him like water. Wonder if I could try hitting it with a . . ."

Vo's transmission ended.

"Mia?" called Petrov. She remembered her mike was off. She flipped it on and called, "Mia? Mia, respond!" She waved Epstein toward the crown. "Joe, go see . . ."

Epstein cut her off: "Going!" He was already scrambling up the icy path.

She got on her scope and sighted down the Omega Station alley where Xray squad was crawling out of the vent and dropping to the ground. The Gremlin zoomed out of the duct, followed by the last man out, Captain Thibideaux. Darox and his Sierra crew had joined them.

* * *

When Thibideaux hit the ground, he pointed at the Gremlin and gestured up the canyon toward Indigo Pass.

"Specialist Hayes, float this junk-box up to the extraction point, and I mean now," said the captain. "Take the rest of the squad for support."

"Aye, sir," said Hayes. He turned to the Gremlin. "Five-two-six, on me!"

The Gremlin drifted toward Hayes. When he started running up the rocky ravine, the drone drifted behind him like a kite on a string. The remaining Xray soldiers jogged behind, guns high in escort.

"Johnny, do you hear me?" called Thibideaux holding his earpiece.

Bradford broke in and said, "Roy, we're downloading the dump right now."

"Good move," said the captain. He turned to Darox. "What's out in the flats?"

"Right now a sleeping Sectopod," replied Darox. "But it'll wake soon, and I expect ADVENT support troops any second." The ground shuddered, and the air shimmered again. "We've also got some kind of psionic artillery exchange going on over the rim up in Roaring Basin."

Thibideaux tapped his earpiece. "Let's get home. All units, full withdrawal."

Then they heard two rifle shots up on the cliff.

"Romeo, what is that?" called Darox, peering upward.

Through the churning snow, he spotted Petrov one hundred meters above them, firing her rifle at a towering, black-helmeted figure on the cliff face. The entity stepped to the cliff's edge, dragging two limp bodies that it promptly tossed over the precipice.

"Good god," said Thibideaux.

Before the ground team could make a move, the tall figure flung its arm upward . . . and then suddenly seemed to fly horizontally along the cliff face toward Petrov.

As the monster glided to Petrov's position, Darox watched her leap off the cliff.

* * *

Petrov jumped without thinking.

As she fell, she heard the Hunter's deep laughing voice call, "Goodbye, Reaper!"

She hit the shallow snow-bowl thirty meters below. By kicking up hard, Petrov managed to stay in an upright position as she plowed another twenty meters downward through the powdery, nearly vertical patch. Luckily, she struck no rocks, and the slide significantly slowed her fall rate.

But when she reached the end of the bowl's gentle outward curve, she shot off the cliff wall with another fifty meters left to the rocky hollow below, where Darox and the others watched helplessly. It was nearly a straight drop, and she clearly saw, as if time's flow had slowed to molasses, how the trajectory curved inevitably to a solid granite slab that would shatter her leg and hip bones if she was lucky enough to land feet first.

I might live, she thought.

And then Petrov felt something strike her back. It penetrated her armor slightly, stabbing her left shoulder blade. She screamed in pain as her body jerked to a bouncing halt in midair.

Then she felt herself slowly lowered.

Darox had his Ripjack claws out before she reached the ground. With a violent swing, he sliced cleanly through the metallic cable attached to a small silver grappling hook embedded in Petrov's shoulder armor.

With a whining *zing!* the cable retracted upward. They all looked up.

An impossibly deep voice called down: "I decide when you die, Reaper."

Then a dark helmeted head with glowing purple eyes leaned over the precipice far above. In a flash, the Hunter produced his rifle, aimed, and fired.

The round struck Roy Thibideaux in the center of the forehead, splitting apart the front of his combat helmet.

* * *

Then things got worse.

Before the captain's corpse even hit the ground, laser fire sprayed the hollow. Darox helped Petrov to her feet, and they both spun to see the Sectopod squeezing out of the alley exit. The walker had to crouch-walk to fit beneath the overhang of the cliff wall, but that didn't stop it from spewing hot laser fire that riddled Drask, dropping him.

"This is Bird One," called a Skyranger pilot over the comm. "We have the drone team, and we are away. Birds Two and Three now at the pickup."

"Go!" shouted Darox to the team. "I have rearguard."

Despite the throbbing pain in her shoulder, Petrov pulled out her Vektor.

"I'm with you," she called grimly, squeezing off a point-blank shot at the Sectopod as it rose up to full height. The bullet penetrated the walker's Wrath Cannon barrel, triggering a small orange flash.

"Good shot!" cried Rika.

Next to her, Mahnk unclipped an EMP grenade and rolled it across the hollow.

"Go back to sleep, you foul machine!" he cried.

The blue pulse did the job, disabling the Sectopod a second time. All three Skirmishers rushed in for point-blank Bullpup blasts. Once the robot finally tilted and clattered to the ground, the team darted away—all ADVENT soldiers, current and former, were painfully aware that "Sectopod death" included a deadly self-destruct detonation.

As the walker exploded, Darox pointed in the direction of Indigo Pass.

"Get to the pickup now, all of you," he ordered, "or I will shoot you myself."

Mahnk and Rika dashed around the rock wall to the rocky ravine that led up to the extraction point. As Petrov followed, she heard a chilling screech behind her. She skidded to a halt and spun to see Darox sprawled on his back with a massive female creature standing over him. Her arms rose slowly, almost hypnotically, a Daisho-style sword in each hand, one long, one short. With swift downward thrusts, she drove the blades through Darox's forearms, pinning both to the granite slab as sparks flew.

Horrified, Petrov raised her rifle and fired without thinking.

It was a perfect headshot.

After the Assassin's head recoiled, she looked stunned for a second, but then she shook it. She turned to Petrov, baring her jagged teeth.

"You assist the hybrid traitor?" she hissed, her voice a metallic screech.

Petrov sighted for a second shot. "Yes, bitch," she snarled.

Releasing one sword, the Assassin extended her free palm toward the Reaper.

"Then you're next," she said.

A purple shockwave hit Petrov and sent her flying. She landed hard, knocked breathless. Her Vektor clattered across the hollow into a crevasse, so she rolled over and tried to draw her revolver. Gasping for air, she watched the Assassin extract the swords and cross them on Darox's neck. But before the alien could slice, the crack of another rifle shot reverberated in the canyon.

Orange blood splattered across the slab underneath Darox's head.

The Assassin shrieked in anger.

"You poach my kill?" she roared.

Petrov heard the *zing!* from the cliff above. Then the dark helmeted Hunter landed next to the Assassin. He gazed down at the fallen Skirmisher.

"So sad," he said with a wicked smirk.

"Perhaps I should take one of yours now," hissed the Assassin and turned to where Petrov lay.

Still choking for air, Petrov pushed to her feet and scrabbled up the steep ravine. As she rounded a sharp curve, she nearly ran into Mahnk, who was descending fast. Petrov seized his shoulder armor.

"Go back," she gasped.

"Is my brother down there?" said Mahnk.

"You can't help him," said Petrov.

Rika hopped down boulders to them. Petrov turned to her and said, "She's coming."

Fear and hatred rippled across Rika's eyes.

Bradford's voice burst loudly into Petrov's ear. *"No more losses,"* he said harshly. "Romeo, Sierra, get to the goddamn pickup."

Rika took Petrov's arm. "The storm is getting worse," she said. "Let's go."

* * *

The Skirmishers helped Petrov climb the ravine to Indigo Pass. There, they boarded the Skyranger designated Bird Two and buckled in. The troop compartment felt empty—just three of them in a cabin built for ten.

As the jump jet lifted off, Petrov gazed through the cabin window at a whiteout snowstorm growing so bad it looked like old-fashioned heavy static on a TV screen.

Next to her, Mahnk sat forlornly. He would not take off his combat helmet.

Across the aisle, Rika stared angrily at her boots.

Petrov was about to speak when a mission briefing monitor suddenly beeped on the cabin's front wall. Then Bradford's face appeared on-screen.

"We don't know yet if this operation was worth what we just lost," he said.

Petrov watched Bradford's face flicker between dark and light.

"But if our Gremlin recovered what we think it did . . . then my old friend Roy Thibideaux is celebrating somewhere in a transverse universe right now . . . with a smoky Kentucky bourbon in his hand."

On-screen, Bradford glanced down at something. He nodded and then looked into the camera again.

"Four minutes ago, we received a field communication," said Bradford. "Somebody calling himself Jeriah transmitted an open channel call that Bird One relayed to the Avenger. He claims to represent a clan called the Templars. They want to talk about joining the Resistance effort."

Petrov glanced at Rika and said, "Well . . . the more the merrier, I guess."

"Yes, but some are merrier than others," said Bradford. He held up a piece of paper. "This is a full transcript of the conversation."

Now Mahnk pulled off his helmet, listening.

Bradford read from the transcript. "'We suffered grievous losses today in Roaring Basin. Our new foe is a product of the Elders, like the other monsters. He calls himself the Warlock, and his psionic power is immense.'" Bradford looked into the camera. "Jeriah also said, and I quote: 'We felt a duty to help your force in the Whitehouse couloir last week.'"

Petrov sat upright. "It was them."

"Yes," said Bradford. "Dr. Marin spoke with Jeriah and verified that fact." He waved the transcript and then sat it down. "These people have great psionic resources of their own, as you well know. If they join our cause . . . and if your mission secured the coordinates we seek . . . well, our future just got two huge shots in the arm."

Petrov exchanged looks with Mahnk and Rika. Then she said, "Let's hope so, Commander Bradford."

Bradford scowled and rubbed the scar on his cheek.

"Soldier, I'm your central officer, not your commander," he said.

Petrov frowned. "What's the difference?"

On-screen, Bradford's face twisted into a half smile.

He said, "If we're lucky, you'll soon find out."

ABOUT THE AUTHOR

RICK BARBA is the author of more than one hundred titles in the film and gaming genres, including books on Star Trek, StarCraft, and LEGO: Jurassic World, to name a few. He lives near Boulder, Colorado.

OTHER EXCITING XCOM2 PRODUCTS FROM INSIGHT EDITIONS:

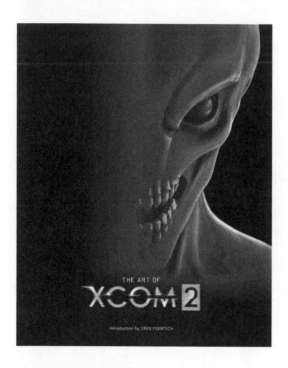

THE ART OF XCOM2

From the developer behind the Civilization series, XCOM is an award-winning, deeply engrossing strategy game. With the Earth under attack by a super-advanced alien race, players command an elite paramilitary organization called XCOM to repel the extraterrestrial offensive and defend humanity. In *The Art of XCOM2*, readers get a behind-the-scenes look at the incredible concept art created for the series and hear from key developers and artists about the challenges, secrets, and rewards of creating this landmark series.

ALSO CHECK OUT:

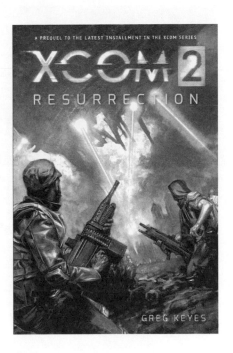

XCOM2: RESURRECTION

In the world of XCOM, the governments of Earth unite under threat of an alien invasion and form XCOM, an elite paramilitary organization tasked with repelling the extraterrestrial offensive and defending humanity. Woefully outgunned, XCOM's only hope is to outsmart and outmaneuver the enemy by turning the aliens' power against them. Making clever use of game elements, *XCOM2: Resurrection* details the strategy and costs of war in a compelling narrative sure to delight sci-fi aficionados and fans of the game series.

AND COMING SOON:

XCOM2: FACTIONS

It's 2035 and the war is over. For two decades, the alien invaders have lived side by side with their human conquests, preaching peace and coexistence, and slandering the human forces that fought to repel them. They think they've won the war. They think this planet is theirs. They think XCOM is finished.

They're wrong.

Set in the action-packed world of XCOM and incorporating elements from the game, *XCOM2: Factions* expands the universe of the successful game franchise. Featuring sharp, dynamic artwork from top comics artists, this original story is the beginning of an exciting new comics series perfect for XCOM players and sci-fi adventure fans.